I0768454

Coastal Midlife Mayhem

By

Brandi Wilde

All rights reserved

This book or part thereof may **not** be reproduced in any form by any means, electronic or mechanical, including photocopy, recording, or otherwise, or by any information storage and retrieval system, except as may be expressly permitted in writing from the publisher as provided by the United States of America copyright law. Requests for permission should be addressed to Swallowtail Productions, LLC,

Attn: Rights and Permissions Dept., PO Box 536, Lewiston, ID   83501-0536.

Unauthorized Reproductions

Warning: The unauthorized reproduction or distribution of this copyrighted work is illegal. Criminal copyright infringement, *including infringement without monetary gain,* is investigated by the FBI and **is punishable by up to 5 years in federal prison and/or a fine of $250,000**. (See http://www.fbi.gov/ipr/ for more information about intellectual property rights.) This book is a work of fiction and any resemblance to persons living or dead, or places, events, or locales is purely accidental. The characters are reproductions of the author's imagination and used fictitiously.

ISBN: 979-8-9914072-1-2

Print Format

Published by
Swallowtail Productions, LLC
Lewiston ID 83501

Cover by
CFM Design

Dedication

This book is dedicated to those authors whose books I've read that have inspired my muse to go off on a tangent into the magickal paranormal world of witches, shifters, and demons. One author, in particular, whom I send a thank you to knows who she is. We've met a few times at conventions, and she's truly been an inspiration to me. Thank you, Tara!

I also dedicate this book to my husband, John, who has put up with my 'multiple personalities' over the years of my writing career. He humors me and makes me laugh, not to mention, he's also helped with the police technicalities of this book. Thank you for always being there for me.

Table of Contents

Chapter 1

Kinsley Bishop hadn't seen her college roommate for several years, and the excitement at seeing her cleared Kinsley's mind of all else but the fun they had back in their college days. Their roommates had partied, but she and Destiny wanted to get out of college with good grades. They had studied hard, and Destiny had gone on to another four years of medical college to become a pathologist specializing in tissue cytogenetics, the testing of tissue samples for organ donors, and was now a doctor in her field.

Since her roommate was a mortal human, there was no way Kinsley had ever let it slip that she had abilities. It wasn't safe to share that information with those who were *mortal* and not part of the witch or shifter community. Mortals had no idea that magick was a way of life, or that Rafe's shifter pack, for that matter, was a real thing. Yet there were some mortals from the federal government who were dead set on hunting down the witches and shifters just in case they were real. Kinsley would keep her community safe no matter what.

She pulled her Yukon into the gravel parking lot and parked near the third cabin, then glanced over her steering wheel as Destiny jumped off the porch and ran toward her Yukon, her auburn hair swaying from her ponytail. Destiny wore dark-framed glasses and looked the same as she had in college. Kinsley got out and met her with a hug, squeezing her tight. "Thank you for coming over to see me. It's always good to see you, granted, not often enough." She held Destiny at arm's length. "You haven't changed a day since we graduated, Doctor Childs!" Kinsley turned her from side to side, admiring her ice blue eyes framed by black-rimmed glasses, definitely a brainy look. She was a beauty queen in her own right.

"Oh, stop. I'm glad I'm here." She looped her arm through Kinsley's. "I needed a vacation and what better place to come than southern Oregon? I love that this little log cabin sits on the shores of the ocean. I can't wait to see the beautiful sunset tonight. It's June and summer has started. The best part is that the weather is warmer down here than it is up in the Portland area!" Destiny turned to view the area around the cabins. "I love the cliffs here. It looks like there's a beautiful home up there overlooking the ocean."

"That's where I live!"

"Shut up!" Destiny's eyes rounded like the puppet, Achmed, making Kinsley laugh.

"Let me grab my purse and the bubbly I brought for us." Kinsley went back to her car. "I brought two champagnes and orange juice for a fun afternoon." She would have ridden her Harley, but she didn't want to blow the champagne corks.

They went inside and soon settled into the Adirondack chairs on the small sunny porch of the cabin to enjoy the warm summer breeze. Kinsley loved the light-yellow cabins, big enough for one or two people. She put her bare feet on the lodgepole railing in front of her.

Destiny went back inside for a bowl of cashews and wine glasses. "Shit, I forgot the ice. Hold on. We can't have mimosas without ice!" She returned in an instant. "This place even has an ice bucket with tongs!" After filling their glasses, Kinsley popped the cork, letting it fly into the yard.

The two giggled and Destiny waved her hand. "I'll pick it up later." She sipped her drink Kinsley poured, sighed, and looked out toward the beach. "How do you live here and not spend every day on the water? I'd have a boat at the marina over there watching all the guys come and go." She glanced at Kinsley. "By the way, how is that hunky sheriff you're seeing? Are things still hot with you two?"

Kinsley rolled her eyes. "Rafe is fine. Yes, we're still hot. His job at the station keeps him busy and the chamber keeps me busy, so we only have the weekends most of the time." Kinsley cleared her mind of the images of Rafe naked in her bed. He did make an impression in her head that was hard to forget.

It wasn't often she took time off in the middle of the week. The Chamber of Commerce didn't have activities she needed to attend, so all was good. "Today is just for you! No work for me today!"

"Thank you, hon. I'm so glad you left that deadbeat five years ago. He didn't deserve you. He was an arrogant ass!" Destiny shivered.

"Hey, didn't you date some hunk back in high school? I remember you still had a crush on him in college, even though you hadn't seen or heard from him. He was a linebacker or something on the football team and built like a wrestler."

Kinsley's heart skipped a beat at the mention of Kai, and she looked out toward the ocean in an attempt to calm her broken heart. They'd only been an item for three years in high school, but the memory of feeling his hard muscles beneath her fingertips was something she would never forget. Nor the way he used to look at her with those blue eyes before he kissed her and held her in his strong arms. Her insides melted every time he was near her. He'd been able to steal her heart back then and had no idea he'd done that...or he would have contacted her.

Destiny leaned forward in her chair and gasped. "Oh, my gawd. You still have a crush on him!"

She looked back at her best friend and bit her lower lip, unable to say a word, but Destiny knew her well enough to read her mind.

"Does Rafe know this?" Destiny shook her head and leaned back in her chair. "Girl, you gotta deal with this. You haven't seen or heard from him since high school. Do you think he's just going to show up here in paradise? I'm guessing you weren't even truly in love with your ex, then either, if your heart was waiting for Kai!"

Kinsley looked out toward the ocean and concentrated on the fishing boats as her heart twisted just thinking of Kai. *Could they ever have a relationship after all these years if he did show up?* "Rafe is aware that I won't commit to our relationship one hundred percent because some guy in high school broke my heart. Rafe doesn't know his name. I'd like to keep it that way."

"I understand. Have you thought about what you would say to him if you ever ran into him? I can't even imagine that if I were in your shoes."

Kinsley looked into Destiny's eyes and saw how much her friend cared. "I think about it every day, Des." She blinked away the tears before continuing. "And no, I never really loved, or felt love, from my ex. Maybe I got married to try and forget about high school crushes. It was a weird relationship that was a mistake for both of us."

She took in a deep breath, hoping to forget. "Regarding Kai, every girl in school wanted their hands on him, but I was the lucky one. So much for that." Kinsley sipped her drink. "I'm not sure where my relationship will go with Rafe. I don't want to break his heart either so I've been as honest as I can with him. He's willing to let me make the decisions on how fast I want us to move forward."

Destiny tipped her head sideways and frowned. "Being single isn't so bad. With the schedule I have at the lab, it's for the best. Brad and I go out occasionally, but his job is time-consuming like mine. He works for the government based out of a Portland office. Having someone to enjoy dinner with is better than eating alone in front of the television."

Kinsley wanted to know exactly what Brad did for the government. That could be dangerous for her witches should Destiny ever become aware of her abilities. She was glad they got off the subject of her ex-boyfriend though. "So, what does the lab have you doing if you're that busy?"

"Last year they put me in charge of the tissue testing for transplants. It's really rewarding when you find matches for those who are so sick. If they don't get the organs they need, shit gets ugly fast. I love what I do, Kins. Often, the testing is at an emergency level, and we have to move fast. The surgeons call constantly to check on results and I love when I can give them good news about a tissue match."

Kinsley certainly didn't envy what her friend did. "It seems like it took forever for you to finish the studies and finally get a chance to work. I'm proud of you, girlfriend. You're kind of amazing. Don't ever forget that!"

A sheriff's patrol car pulled in next to Kinsley's vehicle and her heart sped up a beat. The man was built like a weightlifter, and she often wondered what he saw in her. She caught his gaze through the windshield, and he winked before getting out. He bent to retrieve the cork they had blown out there earlier, held it up, and raised a brow in question as he glanced at each of them.

Destiny looked at her. "Uh oh. Are we allowed to drink outside at these cabins?"

Rafe's deep laugh wrapped around Kinsley's heart as he leaned his forearms on the lodgepole railing by her chair, his seductive blue eyes squinting as he smiled and tweaked her toes. His cologne drifted on the breeze to assault her senses and throw off her thoughts. If he only knew what being near him did to her insides. Why was she hesitating to commit to their relationship when she had the best specimen of shifter material for miles around? Her heart still belonged to a man who had no idea she even existed, and who likely never gave her heart a second thought.

Because you aren't ready to commit! Yet, deep inside, you know that man is never coming back to you!

"This is my college roommate, Dr. Destiny Childs. She busted her ass in college and now does tissue matching for organ transplants." Kinsley saw something sweep Rafe's expression, but it disappeared as fast as it had shown itself. She wondered what he knew that he'd not shared with her and made a mental note to ask him about it. Had he heard of Destiny before?

He reached out his hand to her best friend and something in their touch when they shook hands piqued Kinsley's senses. "It's always a pleasure to meet Kinsley's beautiful friends. Welcome to Pebble Cove, Dr. Childs. I see you two are well on your way to party-stage."

Kinsley sensed a ripple in the air as she watched Rafe and Destiny react to each other. She shook his hand and didn't bother to hide her inspection of Rafe's broad shoulders, the expanse of his chest that nearly popped the buttons of his shirt, and his bulging biceps beneath the long sleeves of his uniform. "Oh, officer, the pleasure is *all* mine! The last thing I want is to be cuffed up in the back of *your* patrol car!" She laughed and Kinsley joined in.

Rafe commanded a male magnetism that seemed to attract all females within range. Kinsley was glad that she held the majority of his attention and enjoyed watching Destiny's reaction to his pull. She was no different than the other females who encountered the man, and perhaps Kinsley was noticing a flirtation that really wasn't there. She dismissed it go for now.

"Do you two have dinner plans? I could bring back a few rib steaks from *Deadly Cuts*. They have the best beef in town."

Destiny's eyes rounded as she turned on Kinsley. "That doesn't sound like a nice place to shop!"

Kinsley loved that idea, since she had left dinner plans open, not sure what Destiny might want to do. She had to laugh at Destiny. "Many of the businesses around here have spooky names, but they do have the best cuts of meat. I think that sounds great."

"It does. I just happened to bring the goodies for salad if that works." Destiny held her glass toward Kinsley, and she refilled it with champagne and a splash of orange juice, along with filling her own.

"Then I'll pick up three steaks, get them seasoned, and be back at four. I'll also bring you more *refreshments*. How's that?"

Again, Destiny's eyes rounded on Kinsley. "Where did you find this hunk who waits on you like that?"

Kinsley smiled and knew she should be ashamed for making Rafe hang around without her committing to their relationship. "He does spoil me!"

Rafe met Destiny's gaze and tipped his chin up. "I have ulterior motives, but don't let that get around. Carry on, ladies...and no driving around looking at the sites after you've been drinking. I'd hate to get a report on you." He leaned over the rail for a kiss with Kinsley and she obliged, watching his ass as he strode back to the car. "Get those eyes back in your head, ladies!" Again, his deep laugh reverberated around them.

Destiny chewed her lower lip as she watched Rafe drive away as if she'd never seen a handsome man before. "Holy shit, woman! I bet he's even hotter when he's barefoot in jeans and a tee shirt. I'd never allow him to wear clothes!"

Kinsley only smiled at her friend. "He *is* molded like no other man, that's for sure."

"I'll bet he *is* molded! You appear well taken care of and that makes me happy."

Kinsley held up her wine glass. "Cheers to the well-endowed men in our lives!" They laughed the afternoon away, walked on the beach, and caught up on their past. Kinsley looked forward to dinner and watching how Destiny and Rafe would get along.

* * * * *

Rafe walked into *Deadly Cuts*, the town butcher shop, and looked at all the steaks, though his preference always landed on rib steaks. A huge side of rib roast lay in the case begging to be cut.

"Can I wrap up a few for you, boss?" Lance Harding pushed his plain-framed black glasses up the bridge of his nose, his bald head glistening beneath the lighting. His steely grey eyes surveyed Rafe.

"Let's do three medium-cut ribeye, Lance." Rafe watched as Lance used one of his long, sharp butcher knives to meticulously slice through the roast like it was butter, and each perfectly cut ribeye folded over onto the freezer wrap. Long fingers carefully tucked the paper as though it contained a precious package, taped it shut, and handed it over to Rafe. Lance had been running this butcher shop since Rafe could remember. The man loved what he did, but he had an odd behavior of perfection that he could only identify as possible OCD. He knew that was a real affliction for some people as he noticed how spotless the butcher shop was. A shiver went through Rafe as he accepted the steaks. "Thanks, Lance. We'll enjoy these tonight."

Lance smiled with a nod as Rafe headed back to his car, but the man always left him with a weird feeling. He was mortal and not of the shifter race. Lance was a thirty-five-year-old family man with two kids and a wife who worked at the shop on the busy weekends. None of his deputies had ever been called out to their place so he didn't know much more about them.

Driving back to his place, Rafe thought back on the electricity between him and Destiny when their hands touched. He'd never reacted like that with another female and his inner wolf had taken notice. He had to try hard not to let his claws out when he touched Destiny, and that surprised the hell out of him. She was mortal, not a witch or another shifter.

Rafe blinked away those feelings and made a quick stop at home to season the steaks, put them in the fridge, and drove back to the station, looking forward to the evening with Kinsley.

As he opened the door to the station, he immediately sensed something was off and he looked around as he listened.

Nate talked on the phone as he stood behind his desk. "I'll grab Rafe and we'll be right out. Thanks, Bryce. Don't touch anything till we get there." He hung up the phone and stared at Rafe. His flexed fingers were covered in fur and his claws were visible. Rafe knew his anger made him close to shifting. If Rafe didn't get him calm, Nate would shift right there in the office.

"Bryce just got in from fishing and landed something that shouldn't have been in the water."

"Fuck!" Rafe's own inner wolf clawed at his guts. "Why can't shit go normal for a while? This is getting crazy. What kind of psycho do we have on our hands? Someone thinks they can mess with our towns and get away with it." His job was to protect their community, but with someone on the loose bent on killing, he had to stop this. "Let's go."

Nate shook off the effects of a near-shift and followed Rafe out to his vehicle, and Rafe drove to the marina down by the rental cabins.

The wooded road toward the boat docks that separated the marina from the cabins seemed especially eerie today, and he blamed that on the recent phone call from Bryce. He was a thirty-something surfer dude who moved up here from San Diego looking for a quieter life. Rafe doubted this was what the man had searched for.

Rafe got out and headed toward the charter office looking for Bryce. He stepped inside the small shack and his gaze went directly to the fifteen-inch metal bracket on the wall that magnetically held about twelve different knife blades. Immediately, his mind envisioned freshly sliced flesh of the victims he'd dealt with already. Rafe shook off the image and met Nate's eyes. He'd also seen the knives. Rafe shook his head and stepped outside.

Bryce met them on the dock as he stood near one of his three forty-foot charter boats. Rafe didn't know where the guy got his money, but his charter company was sought after by those who came here to fish. The younger man had his long, curly blond hair tied back and his dark eyes met Rafe's as they joined him. "I left it netted and hanging on the side of the boat, Sheriff. It ain't pretty. I'm just sayin'...so brace yourself."

With sweaty palms, Rafe boarded the boat with the other two men and Bryce tugged the rope and netting up, dragging the haul over the side until it thudded onto the deck. Rafe swallowed hard on the bile that rose in his throat, hating this part of his job. Bryce pulled the wet netting away as Rafe watched a bloated, naked body take shape. The long dark hair lay tangled in the net as Bryce worked it loose.

Never had he seen such a horrific site.

Again, bile burned his throat. For as long as he'd been in law enforcement, this kind of thing never got easier. The day it did would have to be the day he quit.

The caved-in abdominal cavity appeared to have been ripped away by sharks in about two bites and bloated shreds of flesh hung from what was left. He glanced at Nate. "Get the investigators down here and the coroner on the phone. He needs to tell us what the hell happened here. I want it kept quiet and I don't want sirens."

Rafe gritted his teeth and looked at Bryce. "Nobody finds out about this, got it?" His wolf would have more work if he found out Bryce ever said a word to anyone. Fear among the citizens would cause even more havoc.

Bryce held up his hands. "Yes, sir. I don't need to be told twice."

Nate made the calls to the investigators and the coroner. After the scene was tagged and what little evidence there was taken away, the bloated body was loaded and off to be examined.

An hour later, Rafe drove them back to the station. "Damn, you saw all those knives the same as I did. I know we can't jump to conclusions. We wait for the coroner's reports tomorrow. But tonight, I'm going to enjoy my quiet evening. Kinsley is over at the cabins with her college roommate, and I picked up steaks. Call me if anything else happens tonight, but I doubt the coroner will know anything this soon."

Kinsley met Rafe at the porch of the cabin, took the bag of seasoned steaks, and she kissed him as he wrapped an arm around her waist. She tasted of oranges. He enjoyed the sway of her slender hips as they went inside. Her vanilla cinnamon scent wafted over him. Anytime they were this close, all he wanted to do was hold her, but they weren't alone. He set the bag on the table, then held out two more bottles of champagne and more orange juice. Both women squealed.

"Oh, hon, you didn't have to get us more bubbly but thank you. We finished off what I brought. Destiny has been busy whipping up a salad, and we have potatoes already sliced, buttered, wrapped, and on the coals. The grill awaits you, chef!" She wrapped her arms around his neck to thank him for bringing them food and drink, so he took advantage of her body pressed against his. The front of his jeans suddenly tightened, and he breathed in her scent, hoping to calm down his own body, but to no avail. Rafe nibbled her ear. "Is Destiny's room available for ten minutes?"

"Rafe!" He held her tight for another moment after she squealed, relishing her soft curves as she wiggled in his arms, tormenting his inner wolf. *Just take her now!* He had to release Kinsley before he took her into the bedroom. Memories of their previous weekend still invaded his mind. His heart wanted her for his own but knew it would have to be her decision to fully love him. He'd take her on her terms as long as they could be together.

"Hey, I can step out on the porch and take a bottle with me if you two need time!" Destiny laughed and tried to reach for the champagne.

Rafe gave her a wink of approval, then looked down at a raging Kinsley, her green eyes sparking. "Maybe you can talk her into moving in with me while you're in town!"

She placed her palms on his chest to push away. "Stop! We are sending him outside with a platter of steaks, but he has to open the champagne before he goes out."

Grudgingly, Rafe uncorked a bottle, grabbed a dark beer from the six-pack for himself and went outside with the steaks. To take his mind off sex with Kinsley, he could mull over finding the body in the water instead of fantasizing over what he wanted to do to his woman. No way would he bring up that information at dinner. He'd let Kinsley know about it later.

Before he got out of the door, he heard Destiny's comment.

She giggled. "I'll take his handsome ass into the bedroom if you won't! Damn, woman. I just don't know how you do it. It's a good thing Brad isn't built that well. I'd lose my job because I'd miss so much time at the lab!"

He turned to purse his lips into a kiss toward the women and exited the cabin, laughing all the way to the grill. Setting the plate of steaks on the protruding shelf of the grill, Rafe lifted the lid and carefully placed each steak to sizzle over the coals.

Rafe glanced at the cottage. The crazy sensations he got earlier that day when he shook Destiny's hand would take more time to think on. How could another woman affect him like that if he had such strong feelings for Kinsley? It totally baffled him at this point. Would she have a place in his future? That will remain to be seen.

Chapter 2

As dawn slowly took over the night sky, the truth materialized in the brain about where life had started to go downhill. Those who lived within the glass houses of this sleepy town assumed they were safe and sheltered. One by one, dim lights appeared in tiny windows as the townspeople awoke and soon, they would hear the news that another among them had been found dead. Not even all their money could keep them safe.

No, they would never understand the torment a child endured living a lie within the town where they'd grown up. No one knew the past, being raised here by demented parents who had been highly respected among these townspeople.

Fingers fisted as teeth ground against the other. The cold steel handle of the knife warmed within the tightened grasp.

No one understood.

No one cared.

One day they all would understand why those who suffered deserved a better life. The organs harvested and transported would help so many. The money earned from it would provide a better life for a few.

Oil.

Knives.

Sharpening stones.

My tools of trade.

The slow, smooth, metallic scrape of the blade across the oiled stone sounded like a symphony to the trained ear. With each motion of the knife, the wet blade's edge sparkled, beckoning to be used for slicing through the tender skin of a peach or mango...or removing the tendon from a bone!

There can be no marks within the finished cut.

The sharpened blade must be smooth. Anything else is unacceptable.

It must be perfect.

My parents insisted on perfection...perfect hair, perfect skin, perfect body, perfect feet, perfect teeth. Everything had been regimented for our future upbringing.

Both edges of the blade winked in the light overhead. A finger caressed its length like a sacred tool, but then painlessly severed through the skin.

Bright red liquid spilled over the knife blade.

Damn carelessness!

Mother would be angry over the mess.

Clean it up!

Now!

Wash, disinfect, dry, and store the blades in their proper place.

Always!

Bandage the cut to stop any further mess.

Hot water ran over the metallic blade. Red-tinged water escaped down the drain. The sink and knife were sprayed with bleach and rinsed again. After thorough drying, each one is placed onto the magnetic strips on the wall above the stainless-steel sink. The stone and oil were returned to the drawer, in the exact spot assigned to them.

Turning toward the window, the sunrise created the pink and orange backdrop behind the runners who ran over the beach, their feet leaving messy tracks in the sand.

Pain stabbed at the jawline from the grinding of teeth.

Stop it!

Regain control!

Pain shot through the temples, momentarily blurring any vision.

As the runners moved along, waves swept away the imperfections of the footprint in the sand, making it perfect again.

Deep breathing eased as the sand smoothed, no imperfections.

Peacefulness.

Like mother's face, perfect, no imperfections. Unlike her internal organs that no doctor would help with.

The medical contact would be in touch soon with details of when the next body part collection was to take place. Harvesting organs helped those who needed transplants, unlike the doctors who refused to help mother to extend her life.

The world rights itself in so many ways.

* * * * *

A week later, Kinsley sat outside with her roommate as they contemplated the latest news that she and Angela had just heard from the sheriff. The sunset view overlooking the ocean presented a colorful array of orange, red, and pink as she thought of the gruesome murders. Not much made her afraid, but in the back of her mind, her imagination went crazy with possibilities of what could happen and who was behind all of this. Life used to be so peaceful here in the cove where her home sat above it, overlooking the rocky beach. The clifftop property, an old Victorian two-story, was her retreat for herself and her coven when they held rituals and gatherings, and she was thankful she'd found it out here away from town.

Kinsley rested her head against the Adirondack chair as the warm breeze blew a few strands of hair from her face, thankful that her home was such a peaceful retreat. She looked over at Angela. "I hate that Rafe has to deal with these crazy murders at all. I can't fathom what that does to his mind. Those bodies must be horrific to look at."

Something furry scurried over the grass, up the side of Kinsley's chair and stretched out its long slender body over the warm wood of the chair arm, then looked up at Kinsley. "If you had sex more often with that hunk of yours, he'd have more to think about than these grisly murders."

"Excuse me!" Her familiar ferret never ceased to shock her. Gibbs, as he liked to be called, was a definite smart ass, always speaking out loud what others didn't want to say. Sometimes his advice came in handy, so Kinsley kept him around. He came with the property and normally showed up at inopportune times.

Gibbs shrugged a tiny shoulder. "Hey, just speaking the truth. It wouldn't hurt to have more sex. Am I wrong?"

She leaned away from her ferret and stared at him. "You know that because you have a girlfriend?"

Gibbs cocked his tiny head sideways. "I find it helps take my mind off life's little stresses."

Kinsley ignored his snarky remarks and turned her attention to Angela as she held out her wine glass, needing a refill before Gibbs decided to blurt more craziness.

Angela leaned forward to fill Kinsley's stemless glass with a refreshing, iced Riesling, then refilled her own. "Gibbs, you do bring the comedy. I'm glad you came out for a visit with us." Angela put the bottle back into the ice. "I know we aren't supposed to talk of the details, but it's just us out here. I've never heard of an organ harvester before. Does he really think that is what's happening?"

Just hearing the words spoken out loud created the image of a garbed doctor holding his scalpels. "He does. It hit him hard that the precise cuts on the two bodies were so close to those of a surgeon." Saying it out loud made it more real. Kinsley breathed in the scent from their early fire tonight, hoping it would clear her thoughts of the killer. Weird, she thought of what Destiny did for a living and a chill went up her spine. There was no way Kinsley could do that type of work.

Think of happy things.

She and Angela had worked hard to get the stones set just right for their ceremonial area, along with the cut tree trunks they used for extra stools. The position of the sun was important to their placement of the chairs. The six-foot tall fence they had just painted near the house blocked their space from view, by those driving past, out on the road.

"On a happier note, I love it out here in our secret space." Kinsley ran her fingers down Gibbs' back, over his black and beige spotted fur, and felt him shiver. His little beady eyes looked at her from his tiny beige face that had a darker mask around his eyes like a bandit. His pink and brown nose wiggled the long whiskers.

"Me, too." Angela looked around them. "I'm glad our home is far enough back from the main road, yet wide open to the ocean. Our ceremony area is far enough away from the house, too." She gazed out over the water and the setting sun. Her brows scrunched together as Kinsley met her gaze. "I just received a thought from Suzy, asking if she could pop over."

Gibbs blinked at Kinsley. "Oh goody, a witch party. Let the games begin! I'm outta here. I'll find you later." He chirped at her and scampered off toward the house.

"Sure, I wonder what's up." A few minutes later, as Kinsley finished her wine, Suzy came walking toward them from the gate. Sunset was at least an hour away, so they had time before dark to sit and chat.

Kinsley turned to greet her. "Hey...that was quick!"

A squeal of laughter came from up by the fence as Suzy nearly stepped on Gibbs. Their friend dressed in a brightly colored tie-dyed skirt and yellow peasant top with her sparkly sandals. Her blonde curly hair billowed around her face and down her shoulders. "I teleported! I didn't want to waste time driving out here, and I come bearing gifts!" Suzy hurried toward them. "Besides, Jake didn't want me driving if I was bringing wine." She sat in the other Adirondack chair and dug out her wine cork to open the fresh bottle.

"We can only pray the goddess allows you to teleport back to the right house!" Angela chimed. "Should I run in and grab you a glass?"

Suzy huffed, popped the cork, then swirled her fingers, where a crystal goblet appeared. "I have to use my fancy one!" The wine bottle magickly made the rounds and refilled each of their glasses as they laughed at Suzy's antics. She grabbed it as it floated her way and sat it in the ice bucket. "I'm a little jealous that the two of you share this huge house at the edge of town. Everyone would love to live here overlooking the cliff and beach out there."

Kinsley held up her wine for a toast, proud of her home. "To our secret space when we want to do our spells and rituals without an audience. So, what is so important?"

Suzy tipped her head forward a bit and her brown eyes widened. "Did Rafe tell you they found another body? This one was netted by Bryce while he was out fishing. Doesn't that make two now? Wasn't the other body found down in Hag Stone?"

"Has it been on the news already?" Kinsley gasped. "That damned reporter from KXYZ! He can't hold a story for twenty-four hours. I swear! Down at the Chamber, I've learned not to tell him anything that I don't instantly want the town to know. I'm sure it wasn't Rafe who told him. This is going to kill tourism in our area, and we can't afford that! People come here not only for the hiking, but for the family vacations on the beach and the charter boats to experience the deep-sea fishing by families. We have to save that for the tourists!"

Setting down her glass, Suzy rolled her eyes, gathered, and twisted her hair into a messy bun and clipped it up so the breeze wouldn't blow it in her face. "There! Now, I spoke to Jenna Willard at *Pebble's Cabin Rentals*, and she wants to ward all the cabins to keep her guests safe. And...she also mentioned that one of the handsome guys staying there hasn't returned to his cabin for the past two nights, and he never checked out. I guess he fished a lot and was an avid runner down along the beach. I hope it wasn't him. Jenna said he looked like Brad Pitt and checked in alone, so she has no one to ask where he might be."

The girls sat quietly mulling over the information from Suzy. Kinsley hated that the news would spread everywhere and those who may have been interested in Pebble Cove for a vacation destination would now change their mind. As executive director at the chamber, she didn't want to see her business owners suffer another losing season. Numbers were just now on the rise after Covid had destroyed the beachside town's tourism two years ago.

"Jake said their wolf pack is taking turns patrolling the woods at night. I just don't like this. The killer has to be caught. Maybe one of the pack members will find him and finish him off in the woods where no one will find the body." Suzy chewed her cheek as she met Angela's gaze.

"Do we know the killer is male?"

Kinsley sat forward in her chair as the fire began to die down. She twisted her glass with her fingers. "Rafe said they have no idea if the killer is male or female, but how many female killers have you heard of?"

Angela frowned. "True. We need a mind reader in town to walk around and listen in on conversations!"

Instinct made Kinsley look toward the wooded area as dusk settled in. Something wasn't right in her vicinity. The hairs on the back of her neck tingled. Nothing appeared to move over there, but she couldn't help it. She loved her home and property, yet the woods had always seemed a bit eerie as though bodies might be buried there.

After stirring the coals and sprinkling water over them with the can she kept by the fire pit,

Kinsley picked up her glass. The sun had begun to drop close to the horizon. "Let's head inside before it gets too dark out here. I love living near the woods, but it creeps me out at night. Let's go."

Once inside, the girls settled onto cushioned wicker chairs on the screened porch that spanned the length of the back of the old Victorian house. Angela turned on two lamps which gave the area a soft golden glow that matched the calming scents of vanilla and cinnamon Angela used throughout the home. Kinsley kept up the place, inside and out, with her magick because doing the manual labor wasn't something she wanted to tackle when all she had to do was a renovation spell.

She sat so she could watch the edge of the woods on the far side of her property as the girls chatted. Kinsley hated that she'd been afraid of the dark since she was a child but refused to let it rule her life. The magickal powers she learned from her mom and grandmother helped with that. Her side of the family were fire witches and that had come in handy more times than she could count. She knew some witches had somehow received their powers after forty. It had to be hard not to grow up with it or not have someone to train you properly.

Gibbs scampered up the side of Kinsley's wicker chair, up and over the back to sit on her shoulder, his tiny claws going through the material of her top. She gave him a soft pet. "Did you sneak in the door with us? I didn't even see you."

"You thought to leave me out there with the ghosts in the forest? You know better than that." Gibbs hissed his feelings at her.

"I knew you'd be in sooner or later. I never worry about you, buddy." She ran her fingers beneath his chin and gave him a scratch. "What's the news from the trees?"

Gibbs glanced around at the other witches. "They've heard of the killer that roams the area. None of the trees near us want to see bodies at the base of their trunks."

Again, she stared at the edge of her woods and chewed her upper lip. The eerie sense didn't let up as it tickled the hairs on her neck. Had she actually seen something, or was it just her vivid imagination?

She sent her senses toward the trees.

"Shhh...." Her hand raised toward her friends.

When one of the motion lights went on at the edge of the trees, Kinsley's spine sparked to attention and her shoulders tightened. Gibbs jumped onto her lap, down onto the floor, and ran into the house. "What is out there?"

The two other women stared out toward the woods.

"It could be a raccoon or a deer. Don't jump to conclusions, hon." Angela always calmed her, but Kinsley's imagination ran wild, especially with the recent murders.

Another motion light lit up and Kinsley stood, ready to confront whoever dared to roam her property. "That's it. If we all go over there, the three of us could take care of whatever or whoever that is."

Angela looked at Suzy, nodding her head. "We're in! But Rafe isn't going to like this."

"He doesn't need to know." Angry that someone would prowl around out there on her property and spy on them, Kinsley stomped out the door and across the dark yard, with the other two close on her heels. Stretching out her arms, Angela and Suzy joined hands with her, and she felt the tingle of magick move through their fingertips and up her arms, as they became *one*.

Before they walked half-way across the dark yard, two huge wolves stalked toward them without any hesitation. The glowing yellow eyes threatened her very existence, and she stared back. She squeezed her friends' hands tight. "Hold on, ladies. Power up *now,* and when I let go, step back."

Electricity flowed up both of Kinsley's arms from her coven friends and the power swirled within her. Letting their hands drop, she held out both of her arms toward the intruders and pointed her index fingers. Concentrating directly on them, blue sparks lit up the sky and hit the wolves in the chest as though she'd used a ray-gun, the arc lighting up the edge of the woods. Each one stumbled backward, howling to the heavens. She sent another bolt toward their feet as they ran and disappeared into the trees.

"Holy goddess, Kins!" Angela shouted. "Get back here with us so we can head in. You and Suzy go. I'll keep watching that they don't return until we get in the house. Go!" Angela stood watch while Suzy pushed Kinsley toward the back screened porch and inside.

Chapter 3

Kinsley yanked the screen door shut behind Angela, but still watched the dark wooded area. "What the hell? You know those were enemy shifters, right?" Kinsley shook her head at the audacity of the intruders. "I need something stronger than wine. Come on." Once in the house, she turned the deadbolt on the inside door, headed straight for her wet bar, grabbed the black-labeled bottle of Kentucky bourbon and poured two shots for herself, motioning to her friends. "Grab your own drinks, guys. That was crazy."

The burn she loved followed the golden liquid, and she prayed for protection.

Taking in a deep breath, Kinsley went to look outside through the screened room. All motion lights were dark, letting her know that no one walked around out there. She didn't need that attack with her fears already at the top of the charts. "That has never happened before. What the hell?" She turned back to her friends.

They were downing their own shots. Suzy shook her head as she tried to blow the whiskey sting from her tongue. "Okay, that'll do it for me. I'm heading home before I can't teleport straight! Give me a group hug and call me if something else happens. I can come back." She hugged Angela and Kinsley.

Kinsley gave her one last squeeze. "I'll call if we need reinforcements again."

With a swirl of her magickal fingers, Suzy disappeared, and Kinsley dropped into an overstuffed leather chair in the living room. "I hope the security cameras caught them, but one can't identify who a wolf shifter is. Damn them!" Kinsley had the cameras installed when she bought the two-story three years ago. Nothing had happened since then, so this was too strange tonight. Angela joined her with a tall glass of iced water for each of them. "Thanks."

After dinner and making sure the doors were locked and alarms were set, Kinsley headed up to her room to snuggle in. The old

Victorian stairsteps had small security lights so neither she nor Angela would trip. Angela's room was on the other side of the house, down the hall to the left. When she needed a place to live, Kinsley offered her the spare bedroom, and it worked out for both of them. Best of all, neither of them had to live alone. She liked that.

Gibbs sat at the top of the stairs waiting for her and ran in circles with excitement. "I'm glad you stayed inside tonight, buddy." Kinsley ran her hand over his back, and he followed her into the bedroom.

She'd been fortunate to find such good friends, with magickal powers, when she moved to Pebble Cove. Each of the women in their coven were in their mid-forties and had their own shops. The majority of Pebble Cove had abilities, but not all. The mortals had no clue they lived among a magickal community.

Suzy Jinx owned the *Antiques with Afterlife* shop, and Katie Parker owned the *Krazy Locals Café* where most residents in town stopped to eat her home-style meals. Their water witch, Jenna Willard, owned the *Pebble Cabin Rentals.* Margo Reed was their air witch and owned the *Magick Knots Bakery* that sold the best donuts, bagels, and breads. Katie Parker bought lots of Margo's goods to use in her restaurant, and Jenna bought donuts for the cabin guests.

Angela Proctor's earth elements partnered well with Kinsley's fire elements. Especially in their garden. Angela grew the biggest tomatoes, zucchini, green peppers, and cucumbers she'd ever seen. Together they all combined their talents to keep the town safe. Then again, she'd caught Angela talking to the plants on more than one occasion! Most witches had familiars, but the plants and animals were Angela's. She would say the plants told her gossip from the grass, who heard it from the flowers...who heard it from the bees. Kinsley laughed to herself at her friend's antics. Their garden produced more vegetables than they needed, and Angela canned or froze the extra. She also had her herb garden out back so she could dry them for her *Lotions, Potions, and Spells* apothecary shop. She used one of the extra rooms downstairs as her special kitchen for her herbs and potions.

Yes, her life had seemed calm now that her nasty divorce lay behind her. Her ex hadn't loved her, nor she him, but he dragged it out longer than necessary. Now, her love life was good. She couldn't complain. Rafe treated her like a queen and protected her as best he could, considering she got herself into trouble more times than she could count.

Could I truly fall in love again?

That remained to be seen after Kai had broken her heart. She refused to have it break again. Who would ever guess that a teen-age romance could leave one to never love again. It was her own fault she couldn't move on. After all, she doubted that Kai even knew how deep her feelings for him went. Rafe didn't deserve a woman who couldn't commit totally to him, but he knew where she stood. She breathed in the calming scents of vanilla and cinnamon that permeated the house, and she loved how Angela kept their home smelling so comfortable.

Kinsley had removed her clothes, hung them up, and slipped into her tank top and boxers, then propped up her pillows and sat up under the covers. Gibbs scurried across the comforter and curled up on the other side of the bed next to Kinsley. "Hey, buddy. Glad you found your way up here. I'd hate to think of you outside roaming in the dark. I hate when you do that."

He looked up at her and tipped his little masked head. "But I find things out when I roam around. So, have you and that hunk of yours found time to be together?"

Kinsley closed her eyes and shook her head. "Are you jealous you can't be with us?"

"Of course not. But he does cut into *our* time." Gibbs stretched his tiny feet in the air as he scratched his back on the comforter before curling back up.

Rafe's photo lit up on her phone and her heart raced, like always, when he called. They'd been seeing each other for a few years now but had never moved in together. She preferred her own space instead of depending on a man for her support. Never again would she allow herself to become so dependent on another person. One had to make their own happiness first in order to be happy with others. She reached for the phone, eager to hear his voice to calm her down. "Hey, babe. I missed you today."

"I missed you more. Now...you want to tell me about the intruders you had tonight and why I haven't heard from you?" His deep timbered voice sent shivers through her body, lighting up every nerve it sparked. Funny how he could make her own body betray her when it needed his touch.

Her eyes widened. *Had Suzy snitched on her?*

"I'm a big girl. I can take care of myself, hon." Kinsley knew that wasn't the right answer.

He paused. "That's not the point, babe. There is a lunatic running around right now, and I don't need you zapping every Tom, Dick, and Harry out there. Jake just called me. He said when Suzy popped over, your security lights lit up. I'm glad you have those but..."

The fact that he now had to worry about her, besides being sheriff of the entire county, made her rethink how she behaved. "What could you have done? You don't need to worry about me on top of everything going on at the station right now."

"I'm going to worry. You are on my mind at work or at home. What can I say?"

"Say you'll have lunch with me tomorrow? After we hit the gym in the morning, I have to stop by and see the new owner of *Between the Pages* bookstore, then we can do lunch at Krazy's." She rubbed her fingers over the knotted muscles in her neck. Maybe tonight's events *had* affected her more than she thought. "I wish I had your hands on my shoulders. I'm all knotted up."

A deep chuckle came through the line that ruffled her center. "I can't promise I'd keep my hands on your neck and shoulders."

"Too bad it's so late. We both have to get up early, or we could find out."

His moan sent a shiver right to her core. "Don't push that button, babe. I can be there in a heartbeat."

"No fair shifting to take that shortcut through the woods!" Kinsley knew his wolf form would make quick work of the forest between them. She still hadn't gotten use to that shifter thing. Rafe was pack leader, like his father before him, and that caused him enough stress, in addition to being the sheriff.

She was glad that Nate was his right-hand man...or wolf...at the office and with pack activities. At least he had someone he could depend on.

"I really wish I had you to come home to instead of an empty house. I know we've discussed this before, but I'll keep asking until you give in."

Kinsley couldn't give up her independence even though the divorce was five years ago. She'd fought too hard to be able to live on her own terms with no rules *but* her own. Her ex had controlled everywhere she went, what she did, and who her friends were. As long as they did what he wanted, life remained calm, but should she try to make plans of her own...all hell broke loose.

Never again.

Not that Rafe was anything like her ex, but she wasn't ready to leave her own home for too long. Time really did go by quickly. "Maybe I can stay the weekend."

"I'll accept that, but it's not the same."

The disappointment in his voice stabbed her heart. Did she love him enough to move in for good? Not yet. *Would she ever?* "See you in the morning, hon."

When he hung up, his picture reappeared on her phone and his sexy blue eyes tugged at her heartstrings. *Damn blue eyes anyway!*

Instantly, childhood memories rushed back to her first boyfriend and the teenage crush she'd had on him. Kinsley touched her lips at another memory. No man had ever kissed her the way he had, nor held her heart...or so she thought. *You fool! Lovesick teenagers. That's all it was. He broke your heart and now he's long forgotten about you!*

Memories of him invaded her mind too often. She'd compared every man to him that she'd dated or married and none of them matched his tender lips. *Had she truly been in love with him at so young of an age?* Kinsley wondered how many other women also dreamed of his kisses. The two had lost touch after they split. He had never reached out to her by phone, nor made any attempt to track her down over the years. She tried to move on, but so far, had not found a man to surpass what *he* had made her feel.

Goddess, that was so long ago. Forget him!

After plugging in her phone on the nightstand, she punched her pillow several times before settling in. She begged for sleep to happen and stop the memories.

* * * * *

Morgan Scott looked forward to a life of her own, *her* way, and according to *her* rules. Tired of a humdrum existence, she'd left her ex behind to fend for his own sorry ass. She wanted friends, a place of her own, and the ability to make her own rules of who she spent time with and where she went. Girl's Night Out would no longer be frowned upon!

Touched with a psychic sense, Morgan knew she wasn't nuts and would learn to use this little bit of magick she kept to herself. It seemed to have become stronger as she aged, unlike her older body parts, but she did visit the gym often. This new intuition had to be magical because it warned her to be careful of certain individuals.

Too bad it didn't scream at her twenty-four years ago!

Pebble Cove, a small community on the southern coast of Oregon, had piqued her interest years ago, back when she had stayed at a small rental cottage down by the beach. Her love of books led her to the store she purchased. An old woman wanted to get rid of it and had passed away shortly after selling to Morgan. Now she was certain the sweet old woman's spirit guided her throughout the days...and the nights!

The few friends Morgan made in this tourist village added light to her life and sparked her attitude, not that her sassy tongue needed any help. Although, in her past life, she held her tongue too often toward the snooty friends *he* had. Now it was time for her *new* life.

Some of the shop owners in town were fellow mid-lifers who were perfectly happy living alone on their own. The tourists provided comedy for the locals, and some of them left fun memories. Over the past two weeks, she'd taken breaks from the store to stroll through town to meet some of the other business owners. To her surprise, they made her feel very welcome. The local beauty shop, *Glimmering Touch Spa*, included a few spa services and one day she just might take in a massage. She'd spoken to the gay owner,

Robae Williams, and she had to say, she actually liked his sparkly personality.

Today, Morgan hummed a love song as she grabbed another handful of books to move down to the next shelf when a note card drifted to the floor. Placing the books back on the shelf, she picked up the pristine note and opened it.

I love what you've done with the place. It's almost as beautiful as you are.

...your secret admirer.

Her spine tingled as she held the note. She glanced over her shoulder and around the bookstore, then back toward her coffee corner, looking for who may have placed the note on the shelf. An eerie feeling hung over her. No one looked her way nor paid any attention to her restocking the shelves. Shaking off the creepy feeling, she stuck the note in the back pocket of her jeans. She could reread it later when she had more time to contemplate what it meant. Too many books needed moving to make room for the new arrivals and her stocker had called in sick today. Luckily, the young cashier had come in, giving Morgan time to rearrange the shelves.

She breathed in the smell of the pages as she went back to work. Only a book lover could understand why she owned the store. It certainly wasn't for extra income! Thinking back on the day she walked in here last year, the *For Sale* sign for *Between the Pages*, had caught her interest. With small town charm, nestled among other store fronts, the window offered a peek back in time with shelves of books and gift items.

The old woman she'd bought the store from could barely walk. The small-town store had been in the woman's family for years and she hated to sell it to just anyone...especially not to someone who wanted to tear it down. Living above the store forced the poor old woman to climb those stairs several times a day, and she just couldn't do it anymore.

The bookstore was the perfect business for her. Being a single mom for the past five years, and in her early forties for Goddess sakes, had forced her to work long hours, leaving her son to be alone too often. Teenagers could be a pain in the ass, but she had to give Logan a break after the divorce they had just been through.

With a little luck, he'd graduated college and agreed to move with her to Pebble Cove until he found a real job. A fresh start would give them both time to reconnect and make new friends here. Logan had found an apartment to be on his own with money he'd saved working through college, but he did help out at her coffee cafe for extra income. Time had passed too fast as she remembered his growing years. Soon, he'd be off on his own for good. He'd gotten his degree in veterinarian medicine and was waiting to schedule his licensing exam. He wanted to work with a local doctor, if he could, to get his start. Morgan was proud of the man he was becoming.

Wiping a tear from her cheek as she pushed away thoughts of her past, there were still so many books to rearrange. If only the books would just slip onto the shelves, in the proper order, it would save so much time. When her fingers tingled, she flexed both hands and gave them a shake. The air around her sparkled with light and suddenly all the books were on the shelves, and in the proper order!

Morgan gasped and looked around. *How could this possibly have happened?* No one seemed to have noticed what took place. She looked at the empty boxes on the floor and then at the shelves. All the books were exactly the way she had envisioned the finished job. She walked to the end of the shelf and peeked around the corner, half expecting the old woman's apparition to be standing there.

With a shake of her head, she knew it was time for a break and some lunch. She looked up as a woman come in the door. The beautiful green eyes drew Morgan in and made her feel comfortable immediately.

"Hi. I'm looking for the owner of the bookstore."

"That would be me." A slight spark of electricity in the air around them made the hair on Morgan's arms stand up, but she dismissed it to be the old woman's spirit. Certainly not something this new stranger would give off. "I'm new in town and bought the store a few months ago."

"I'm Kinsley Bishop, the Executive Director of the Chamber of Commerce. I always like to let the new business owners get settled in before I stop by to welcome them to Pebble Cove." Kinsley looked around. "You have changed a few things since the previous owner sold. I like it. The coffee area gives it a warm touch."

"The customers really enjoy it. I painted it a bright color to add some cheer. I almost feel like the previous owner is here with us in spirit. I know she loved owning the bookstore." Morgan admired the confidence the director had. More important, Morgan remembered all the names from the Salem witch trials from her history classes, and Bridget Bishop had been the first to be hanged. *What a coincidence! Could she be a descendant?* Ms. Bishop wore her long dark hair in a ponytail and a stunning pencil skirt with a sweater and heels and had a way of making one feel at ease.

"I'm in charge of getting new business owners to join our chamber. We have networking meetings once a month, and it allows you to meet the other owners in town. You'll fit in well. I'll leave the membership form with you. The dues can be paid online or mailed in. Whichever you prefer. This calendar shows the monthly happenings and our meeting times. I'm glad I got to meet you today. Again, welcome to our little piece of paradise."

Chapter 4

After Kinsley Bishop left, Morgan thought about the magick she felt earlier when the woman had arrived.

Was it just her imagination?

Impossible. It had to be the old woman's spirit.

She got back to work breaking down the empty boxes, still unsure what the hell had happened and how the books moved on their own. Now she needed to work on the box of new books that arrived yesterday and carried them to the small table. Her customers would see them on the display as soon as they walked in the door. The smell of new books made her happy.

The bookstore bustled with shoppers today looking for that special something among her gift shelves. Morgan glanced toward her small coffee shop and smiled again. Customers occupied several tables in the back corner drinking lattes and reading around the gas fireplace she had installed for that homey feel she wanted to portray.

A few hours later, the tiny bell on her door chimed and she turned to welcome the new customer stomping the rainwater from their boots before coming further into the store. "The coastal weather out there is crazy in April! At least I know I can warm up in here with a mug of your coffee!" The jovial sixty-year-old woman unzipped her coat, loosened her scarf, and rubbed her hands together.

"Jennie, you bring warmth with you every time you visit us."

Jennie leaned toward her. "Well, the chilly weather is hell on the joints, but your fireplace should fix me up. Unpacking new books again, eh? Stacy has my new one at the counter. It came in, and I can't wait to read it. I have an hour before the children arrive for story time!"

"The kids love having you read to them. Thank you." Morgan hugged her. Jennie had been doing the children's story hour for a few months, giving the parents time to shop and enjoy coffee while their children listened to Jennie read.

Morgan knew she had been blessed with many new friends who welcomed her when she moved into town. She thought about sassy, sarcastic Suzy Jinx, who owned the antique shop down the block. The middle-aged woman swore her place was haunted, but said she had magickal powers to ward them off. Morgan would have to become friends with her so she could learn more about what type of magick she talked about. Perhaps she could learn more about her own abilities...abilities she had no idea she even had.

With the new book table all set up, and the old ones in their place on the shelves, Morgan decided to walk a block down the street to Suzy Jinx' shop. The employees would be fine on their own. Morgan grabbed her umbrella and off she went. Too many questions swirled in her mind about what had happened today and who better to talk to than Suzy. Logan would think she'd lost her mind if she mentioned it to him.

The cold salty breeze off the ocean brought drizzling rain and along with it, the slight smell of fish from the cove where the trawlers docked. She quickly made her way down the block, holding tight to her umbrella. One would think it would be warmer being this close to the California border. Glad for the canopy outside the shop of *Antiques with Afterlife,* Morgan opened the door and heard the silver bell jingle at the top.

"Oh my gosh, I'm so glad you popped in today, Morgan." Suzy's blonde curly hair was in a messy bun, which looked great on her and even a bit sexy. The woman was gorgeous with her soft brown eyes and bright smile.

"I needed a break and what better way to clear my head than to come browse and chat with you?" Morgan closed her umbrella and leaned it near the door. She hugged Suzy but the tingle Morgan felt when they touched surprised her, and she stepped back.

"Tell me you felt that, too?" Suzy's eyes rounded in her heart-shaped face.

"Umm, I did. It's happened a few times today." She took in a deep breath, hoping it would clear away the tingle.

"It's the magick!" Suzy's eyes sparkled with mischief.

"Excuse me?" Morgan looked around the shop with a hope that no other customer had heard the crazy comment.

"Are you not aware of your own magick?" Suzy waved her manicured hand. "It's okay. Some of us have it happen like that. One day you're normal and the next day…you're not! You've had weird things happen in the past few days?"

Morgan looked around the shop again but didn't see any other customers.

"Don't worry. We're alone and it's a good thing. You need to talk to someone, which is why the magick brought you here. Come over to the back corner table and let's talk. I think you have a lot of questions."

How does she know all this? Morgan took a chair and relaxed, eager for answers.

"I know because I can sense what others feel, like an empath, and I'm a bit of a mind reader. I think you have powers you aren't even aware of."

Morgan sat at the table with Suzy. "This is too strange, but here goes. My first question would be about the *wards* you said that protect your store."

Suzy spread her fingers out flat on the table as if she felt something from the wood. "Was your mother a witch or your grandmother?" Her warm eyes met Morgan's.

"Neither that I know of. Is this something that is real?"

Suzy leaned back in her chair and let out a hoot. "Oh dear!" She composed herself and leaned closer. "I don't mean to laugh. Yes, magick is real, but the humans don't believe in it. When one has abilities, we keep it hidden when they are around. I'm guessing something has happened to bring you here today, so tell me about it. And don't think I'll laugh at you because it was a fluke."

Morgan bit her lip, contemplating how to go about explaining it all. "I'll just blurt it out. I was reorganizing the bookshelves to make more room and thought how much easier it would be if they just popped onto the shelf and organized themselves." She stared at Suzy. "And it just happened! They flew everywhere! The books were all correct, the boxes were empty, and I just stood there in shock. I had to look around to see if anyone else saw it happen, but no one did." Morgan leaned back, giggled, and crossed her arms. "Tell me how that happened!"

Nodding her head, Suzy acted like it was normal. Morgan didn't feel anything like *normal.*

"That's all you need to do. Imagine what you want to accomplish, and wham...it happens. Just a wave of your hand usually does it. Did your fingers tingle?"

Morgan widened her eyes. "Yes!"

Suzy reached out and laid her fingers on Morgan's arm. "Sometimes, as we get older, magick comes into play after we turn 40." Suzy pulled her hand away and crossed them on the table. "Mine didn't happen that way because my mom knew early on that I had abilities, so she worked with me, taught me the spells I needed, and passed on the family grimoire of spells. Each family has one. I would guess someone in your family has it."

Leaning on the table, Morgan thought about who she may have gotten her powers from. She would have to call her mom and demand answers. Her son Logan, so far, had not shown signs of magick nor told Morgan of any incidents. She was unsure if she needed to have a talk with him, so he wasn't shocked if something strange happened, like it had to her earlier today. She didn't want Logan to feel he had to hide anything. "I'll have to make a few phone calls. Until then, how do I figure out what happens next? And how do you conjure wards to protect your shop and what do you protect it from?"

"I'm sure you're aware that it's possible for objects to carry the spirit of its previous owner. Sometimes those spirits have evil intentions. Since my shop is full of antiques, many items have spirits connected to them. I create a ward spell to protect my shop from the spirits intent on evil. I reaffirm that spell monthly so that my husband and I remain safe from all of them, and they don't follow me home."

Morgan had even more questions swirling in her head than she did before. "It's a lot to take in and understand it all. That I'm able to do any of those things is unknown to me. I wish I'd known about this while I was married, I could have turned that asshole into a toad!" Morgan sat straight in the chair. "I had a visitor today that caused a tingle of something like electricity, but I thought it might be the old woman's spirit."

Suzy shook her head. "Who came to see you?"

"The executive director of the Chamber."

"That would be Kinsley Bishop. She's one of us and our coven leader. She's our High Priestess." Suzy tipped her curly-haired head to the side. "I would like you to come to one of our meetings where you could learn more about our witch community. We are happy to help you learn what your family didn't teach you."

"There are other witches in town?" Now Morgan was blown away. "How have I never known witches existed?"

"We don't carry signs, hon. There are more than just witches living in Pebble Cove." Suzy reached over and rubbed the back of Morgan's hand.

"I'd love to be able to learn. Who else in town is in your group?"

Suzy chewed her cheek before answering. "We are a coven of witches. Izzy, the old woman who owned your store, was one of us, in case you've felt things in your apartment.

The girls would be thrilled to have you join us. We're getting together tomorrow after work if you want to come by and go with me."

"I don't want to intrude, but I'd love to meet the others. Thank you so much!" Morgan debated with herself about the note and whether to bother Suzy about it. She reached into her back pocket. "I want to show you something that fell from one of the bookshelves today. It's kind of creepy."

Taking the note, Suzy opened it, read it, then glanced up to meet Morgan's gaze. Her eyes held suspicion and Morgan's spine shivered again.

"You don't know who wrote this? I don't feel right about it at all."

"When I found it, the store was full of customers, yet none of them were looking my way. You'd think one of them would notice that I found it, but they were all reading or shopping." Goosebumps rose on her arms, and she rubbed them away.

Suzy handed her the note back. "Let me know if you get anymore notes. We might have to let Nate know something isn't right. He's the town deputy at the sheriff's office."

Morgan put the note back into her pocket and stood up. "I'm glad I came over. You've helped me a lot. I will be back tomorrow after the store closes to join you for the meeting. Thanks again."

Suzy walked with her to the door and handed her the umbrella. Something in the area tugged at her inner soul, assaulting her like never before, as though a strong sexual power called to her. Morgan looked behind Suzie, wondering if a ghost had followed them to the door and wanted to leave with her. Nothing visible showed itself and she tried to shake off the strange feeling.

As Morgan opened the door to leave, a deputy was walking past the *Antiques with Afterlife*. When he made eye contact with Morgan, something passed between them that equaled the feeling she had before she turned around to leave. She couldn't put her finger on it, but there was a connection she couldn't ignore. His gaze took her in slowly from head to toe and then once again met her eyes. The sexual pull in his eyes was like none she'd ever experienced before. As if he'd reached inside to caress her heart.

Suzy stepped out the door. "Nate, how are you today? Have you met Morgan yet? She owns *Between the Pages* bookstore."

He stopped to hug Suzy and held out his hand to Morgan. She still stood mesmerized by a man she'd never met. When she felt his firm handshake, he held hers a bit longer than necessary and she had to pull away first as energy sparked up her arm. Today had too many occurrences for her to ignore them all and she wondered what was happening.

His smile drew her attention as it went to his eyes. Nate had one green and one blue eye, but they were both light enough that one didn't notice immediately. His dark hair wasn't cut short, but it wasn't long, reminding her of a dark-haired Chris Hemsworth. The deep-set eyes called to her.

"Glad to meet you. I'll have to make a point of stopping into the store. But on another note, I want you both to be fully aware of your surroundings when you're out and about. Another body was found last night. I'm sure it'll be on the news, but I wanted to be sure you knew, Suzy. Please be careful and be on the lookout for anyone who stands out to you."

Morgan met Suzy's gaze, and she knew Nate should hear about the note. She explained what happened, showed the note to Nate and he asked if he could take it back to the station. "Just be aware of your surroundings. Are you heading back to your store? I'd be happy to walk you back."

"I'd like that." She walked back with Nate while he told her how long he'd been with the department after he left the marines.

Once at her store, she thanked Nate and reluctantly went up to her apartment. She would have liked to have a longer conversation, but the late hour made her rethink that. Nate had other rounds to make before he was off duty.

The employees would close the place up. Right now, she just wanted to get upstairs and lock her doors. Her employees would hear the news tonight and her coffee shop would be buzzing in the morning. She knew Logan would be working and would keep the coffee flowing as they chattered away. The customers loved the different coffee flavor combinations he whipped up for them. Her son got along with people, and he enjoyed trying new flavors for holiday drinks.

She closed and locked the door, then leaned against it. Had she just imagined that Nate's soul called to her own? Impossible. There was something between them that she didn't quite understand, but her intuition screamed at her to learn more about Nate.

A small lamp that Morgan always left on next to her sofa allowed enough light to see when she entered her tiny apartment. Each night it seemed there was an aroma of the old woman's perfume that gave her comfort and washed away a bit of loneliness.

"Hi, Izzy. I'm home. Thank you for watching over the place today." Morgan felt as though she didn't live alone and enjoyed thinking Izzy was always there with her. She set her umbrella in the corner and hung up her jacket. Life made her smile at being able to put her feet up and not have to do anything if she didn't want to.

Yesterday was dust and vacuum day, which didn't get done. Out of curiosity, she closed her eyes and thought about it all being done. Then she opened her eyes, twirled her hand in the air and a breeze blew past her as her magick cleaned up the dust and dirt on the now sparkling floor.

Astonished, she assumed Izzy had just done that. "Thank you, Izzy. I love the help!"

She grabbed a soda from the fridge and then turned on the news to hear what had happened in town today. After she put her feet on the ottoman, the television flickered twice, which it had never done before, then the lights blinked. Morgan looked around. "Izzy? Are you just letting me know that you're aware of what's happening in town?"

The lamp flickered and she tried to calm herself as the news report flashed its red banner for the breaking news alert. The news anchor told of the body found by Bryce and stated the public needed to be aware of their surroundings. Morgan wished she'd turned on another lamp. When she pointed at it, the lamp turned on. "Holy goddess!"

The air around her seemed to sizzle. Her attention went to the overstuffed chair beside her, and an apparition of Izzy sat there with her feet up. Morgan froze, never having seen an apparition before. She wasn't afraid. Shock would be a better word.

"You are coming into your powers. I like that. I knew you were special the day you came into my store."

"How? How have I not seen you before this?"

Izzy cackled and pulled her shawl tighter around her. "Because you didn't believe in yourself. After today, you now have knowledge of your abilities, so I knew you would see me. I've been here since you moved in, my dear. And I know you have many questions, but...you must first make that call to your mother. I'm not going anywhere. I'll always be around for you."

"It comforts me to know you're here. I have so much to learn."

"Your mother has the family grimoire that you need to get your hands on. That will help you with the spells you need to be aware of. Premonitions are what you can concentrate on now. But be very careful with it."

"What does that mean?" Confusion clouded Morgan's mind. So much to learn, yet her mother never said a word.

Izzy just shook her head. "All I can do is advise you to get the grimoire, my dear. You have such a wonderful future ahead of you."

With that, Izzy disappeared, leaving Morgan a bit shocked. Knowing she needed answers, she picked up her phone to call her mother and get to the bottom of things.

Chapter 5

Nate parked his patrol car and took Morgan's note into the station with him. He'd been with the sheriff's department for fifteen years, and they never had trouble with murder in this area. Now they had found a second body in six months.

Rafe was the sheriff and one of the best bosses he'd ever worked for. He sat in his office with papers scattered over the desktop. His brows knitted together as he scoured the information in front of him. Nate leaned against the doorframe. "Any more news or breaks in the case?"

Rafe leaned back in his chair; his lips pursed in frustration. "We need to figure out who is doing this. Why the hell are body parts missing from each of the victims? And then there is the crazy pack member, Bobby Joe, who went missing. His backpack was found in the park by the beach, but nothing else, and no one has seen him for days. Jenna called earlier to say one of her cabin renters also hasn't been around for two days, yet his locked car is still in front of his cabin."

Pulling out a chair, Nate sat in front of Rafe's desk and threw the note over so he could read it. When Rafe looked up and met his gaze, the anger burned hot in his blue eyes. "Where did this come from?"

"The new owner of *Between the Pages*. She said when she was reorganizing the books today, they fell from the shelf. That's all she knows. None of her customers paid any attention when she found the note, so she put it in her back pocket. Suzy Jinx is the only other one who knows about it." Nate kept it to himself about the reaction he had when he met Morgan. He couldn't figure out the strong sexual pull himself, and until he understood what it was, he'd keep quiet. Her scent was immediately attractive to him, and his inner wolf tried getting his claws out. Luckily, he'd been strong enough not to let that happen in front of Suzy and Morgan.

"And she'll let us know if she receives another note? We really don't need this nut job roaming free. The coroner said once he got inside the body that Bryce found, he saw precise cut marks, not just torn flesh from a shark bite. The heart had been cut out before the body was tossed in the water. Both bodies had missing internal organs, although different organs were missing in each body. Too strange. The precision with how they were removed is uncanny. As if it were a surgeon who cut them out."

"That's eerie. Organ harvesters come to mind. I hear there's big money in that. Let me know what I can do." Nate would be sure to check in with Morgan in a day or so. He'd investigate the customers who frequented her store, too. Perhaps he needed to stop in for a coffee occasionally. That would give him reason enough to make an appearance.

"We need to make sure several of the pack members can keep their eyes on the beaches and the wooded areas from Ravensville to Pebble Cove. It wouldn't hurt to have a few prowl around Ravensville. I don't want anything missed." Rafe looked up at the area map and the location pins he'd put into place. "One body was found in the woods down in Hag Stone. One of these people may have stayed in the rental cabins down by our beach, so I think they're just random kills. Morgan, on the other hand, is singled out by the note writer. I don't like that at all in my town."

"I'll call Diablo and get his crew out to watch the wooded areas and shorelines. His guys are good and they're loyal." Nate went to his desk to call Diablo at the bar in Hag Stone. The packs in the three local towns were comprised of wolf, cougar, and bear shifters and the tension over the last three months had everyone on edge. He had even helped in the watch-shifts, prowling about the areas, but hadn't seen anything strange or even humans roaming about in the dark.

Rafe walked past Nate's desk. "I'm on my way over to Kinsley's office at the chamber to see how she's doing. The tourism numbers have been down some since the murders are making the news, and she's taking it personally. I'll see you in the morning."

* * * * *

Rafe pulled up to the old brick building where Kinsley's office was. The place was a hundred years old and had a bloody past. A chill crawled over his chest as he thought about the old murders. He pushed his car door shut and headed inside, but not before his wolf stirred at unseen forces. Rafe stopped for a moment just inside the door of the old structure. A foul odor was faint, but he smelled it as he looked around. The old stairway that led to the lower level was chained off to the public, but spirits were free to roam should they choose. A muscle twitched in his shoulder as he walked toward the Chamber of Commerce. He'd have to ask Kinsley about the odor later.

He said hi to the receptionist at the chamber as he went toward Kinsley's office. Her door was open, but he still knocked. Her smile lit up her face, and her green eyes sparkled. She wore her hair in a ponytail today, and it hung in soft curls down to the middle of her back. His first thought was to release the band binding her hair to watch it fall over her shoulders.

"Hey, handsome!"

"Are you working late tonight, or would you like to drive with me to Hag Stone and get a drink so we can chat with Diablo?"

Kinsley's shoulders gave a slight slump. "My coven has scheduled a meeting at my place tonight. They're a bit on edge and want to be sure we're all on the same page with the shift in the air since all this is happening. Can I get a rain check?" She turned off her computer screen, laid two pens side by side for tomorrow, and grabbed her purse.

"Anytime. I'll walk you out if you're ready." His eyes went to the curve of her hip and slender thighs in her tight pencil skirt...and those heels. He took in a deep breath, wanting to take her in his arms right here and feel the warmth of her lips. Her green gaze met his with disappointment in her eyes that she couldn't go with him tonight.

She turned off the office light, said good night to her receptionist, and took Rafe's hand as he led the way to her car. "I appreciate you checking on me. When the coven meeting is over, I'll give you a call. What I hope to work on tonight is getting them used to using their magick for self-defense should they need it and not second-guess themselves. That's how shit happens. Some of them are good at self-defense and can help me teach those who need it."

Rafe opened her car door and did his damnedest to keep his wolf under control. Her vanilla scent assailed his senses, tempting him to take her right here at her car. He took in another cleansing breath with his claws threatening to touch her back if he didn't tame it down. His fingers held tight to her door. "I know that Suzy and Jake train at the gym. She should be a good trainer. Let me know if you want some of us out there to help."

Kinsley leaned close and kissed him, just not long enough as he memorized her scent yet again. "That might be a great idea. I'll let the girls know that's an option. Stay safe out there, hon. Say hi to Diablo for me." She climbed in, and he shut the door.

Rafe watched her drive away and headed for his car, calming himself and shaking out his arms. Hopefully, he could run the forest tonight to relieve some of the tension. He would call Diablo and run with his pack for a change. Rafe knew Kinsley would call, but he had a few hours until that time.

* * * * *

When Kinsley got near her home, she hit the button that opened the tall eerie, iron gates to her driveway, and she loved them! Each gate had tall iron spikes that held a dragon on an ancient circular shield that gave an ominous appearance to the place. They were a perfect addition to the Victorian home.

Once inside, she changed into her yoga pants, tank top, and sweatshirt. That should keep her warm enough for their meeting in the screened room tonight. Some of the coven members were itching to hone their talents and become better.

As she made her way down the stairs, the scent of vanilla and cinnamon floated through her home from the candles. Kinsley found Angela finishing up a body lotion since she created her own with essential oils, coconut oil, and lavender and other herbs from the garden. The mixing beaters hummed away, so Angela didn't hear her come into the kitchen. Rather than scare her and have lotion fly all over the counter and cabinets, she called out to Angela. "Whatever you're mixing up smells wonderful!"

"I had to make a new batch of my face cream. I only have two jars left at the shop. My customers crave this magick in a jar. They just love it." She turned off the beaters and came at Kinsley with a finger full of lotion. "Come on, Kins, let me test this on your neck. You're going to love it!"

She took a step backward as she held up a hand. "I love all the potions and lotions you create, hon." Kinsley knew Angela wouldn't stop until it was lathered over her skin. She pulled down her sweatshirt collar and held her neck out.

Angela gently smeared a dab on her skin. "Now rub that in and feel the tingle! Maybe I should mix up something for the guys to get a tingle, too!" She tipped her head back and let out a laugh.

Kinsley smoothed the lotion into her neck and loved the way it made her skin feel. "It does tingle a bit…and it smells wonderful!" She laughed at Angela's comment. "Maybe you need to have a shelf for sex-aid potions and lotions!"

Angela's face changed two shades of pink from her neck up to her cheeks.

With wide eyes, Kinsley took in a huge breath. "Oh, my goddess! You already have a shelf of them, don't you!" The two of them laughed together and it felt good to let go of the day's anxiety of business. "I guess I need to come into your shop more often and look around at what you actually have for sale. Will I be shocked?"

"I'm not answering that. I have gift bags for those purchases so no one else will know what you buy!" She cleaned off her beaters, not wasting any of the lotion and scraped it into the bowl, which she covered with clear plastic wrap until she was ready to package it. "I'm also not saying *who* visits my shop and buys me out of those sexy lotions." She glanced over her shoulder begging Kinsley to ask who her customers were.

Kinsley held up a hand. "Nope. I don't want to wonder who and how they use those. Just stop it." She opened the fridge in search of a snack.

"I made us a nice salad for dinner before the girls get here. I love that we both enjoy everything in our salad and that we prefer iceberg lettuce and not those other leafy greens some use. Ewww! There is also shredded cheese, sunflower seed topping with cranberries and nuts, and lots of bacon bits."

"You always seem to read my mind for what I'm hungry for. I love you and so glad you're here with me." She pulled the items from the fridge while Angela cleaned up her mess. They had big crystal salad bowls so they could enjoy lots of goodies and croutons. "I talked to Rafe tonight as I was leaving the office. He offered to have a few of the pack members come over and help workout with the girls for hand-to-hand combat so they would be ready for any emergency. Unlike the catastrophe that happened six months ago when the California coven showed up thinking they could take over our territory here."

Angela put away her supplies and sat down to eat. "Suzy called today. She hoped it would be okay if she brought a woman just coming into her abilities and has no idea what is happening with herself. Her name if Morgan Scott."

"I met her today. She's the new owner of the bookstore that Izzy sold. Goddess bless her soul. You know, when I shook hands with her today, I did notice magick around her. I didn't say anything since some don't like others knowing, but those of us with powers can sense it. That would be why she didn't say a word. If she is new to this, she isn't aware of how it all works." Kinsley loved the salads Angela prepared for them and enjoyed a bite of tomato and cucumber drenched in tangy Italian dressing. "So, did you cut all this up or did you just swirl your fingers? Not that it matters!" She laughed because even though Angela could use her magick, she seldom used it for tasks like making dinner.

Angela gasped but laughed. "I cut everything up, thank you. Now, cleanup will be a whirl of my fingers, but I do enjoy cutting the veggies."

With the coven meeting in thirty minutes, Kinsley gathered the white candles and sage so they could cleanse the area before they started. Angela always took care of that for them, so Kinsley put them aside and ready, along with her small dish and white feather. Additional chairs were brought in, and she set out the wine glasses for the girls who usually each brought wine.

The coven meetings were fun, and knowing they would be helping Morgan Scott tonight would be even better. She remembered when she came into her own abilities and how scary that had been. Her mom had warned her ahead of time and had been there to help her learn how to use them for good and never for her own benefit, like bringing love into her life. Messing with the free-will of others was a no-no.

Suzy and Morgan were the first to arrive, followed by Jenna, Margo, and Katie. Once they filled their wine glasses and niceties were done, Angela lit the sage, tipped it lower to burn for a minute and then blew it out to smolder in the dish. She took the white feather to push the smoke into each corner of the screen room to expel any outside entities. This was done to protect them all and keep them safe.

Kinsley welcomed Morgan to the group. "We're glad you chose to join us and please know that you are among friends. Nothing comes between our sisterhood. Anytime you need to call for help, each of us are here for you. Always remember that." Kinsley looked at each of her sisters to confirm her words, and each nodded. "Are we all in agreement for Morgan to be a member of our sisterhood and depend on each other?"

In unison, they each replied, "We do."

Morgan's knee bounced as they sat close together. "I don't feel like I am as magickal as each of you. I'm only just learning that I have abilities and not sure why my family never enlightened me. So, I'm a bit confused, but willing to learn from each of you. Thank you for allowing me to be a part of your coven."

Suzy reached out to curl her fingers on Morgan's arm. "I have spent a little time with Morgan, and I think she has abilities that will serve us well if we can tap into what she is capable of. On another note, I think we should all be aware of the possible danger that could crop up at her bookstore. Just the other day, she found a message that someone left for only her to find." Suzy told them what the note had said. "I think we all need to be alert in each of our places of business and be on guard with those who visit us. Deputy Nate has the note, and they are now aware."

Kinsley's eyes widened at the audacity of a stranger leaving such a personal note. "I wish you could have confided in me when I was there the other day. Please let me know if you get another note. I don't like that we have someone in our town making us afraid to do anything." She knew it wasn't her fault, but she wanted to be able to help everyone.

"It was a bit jarring, to say the least. I want to learn more about how to protect myself from things like this. I should have seen it coming." Morgan rolled her glass between her palms.

"We can't always see things that want to harm us. You will learn as you go," Angela advised her.

"Well, the other day, I was wishing my books could just shelf themselves and be organized. The next thing I knew, the air felt different, and my fingers tingled, and…the books all of a sudden were on the shelves in the proper order. I was shocked and looked around to be sure no one saw that."

"In your mind, you envisioned what you wanted and made it happen. That's all it takes, so be careful what you wish for, and never use it for selfish reasons or personal gain, such as wishing money to come your way," Jenna said.

"That's really all I need to do?"

Suzy squirmed in her chair as though she had a secret to share. "Morgan, set your glass down to free your hands. There you go. Now, envision your favorite book you might have at home. Get a good vision. Now, with a wave of your hand, hold it out flat."

Everyone watched with interest as Morgan made a small wave of her hand, held it out flat and as though upon command, the book lay across her palm.

"Oh, my goddess!" She grabbed the book with both hands so it wouldn't fall to the ground.

With eyes wide open, she glanced at Kinsley, then at each woman around her. In turn, they smiled back at her. Kinsley was proud that Suzy could teach Morgan. "Very well done. How do you feel?"

Morgan turned the book over in her hands, then fanned the pages. "It's the book I had on my nightstand next to my bed. How..."

Kinsley shrugged a shoulder and gave her a smile of approval. "That's just how it works.

We'll help you learn the basics. I'm sorry your parents never thought you needed to learn this. Normally witches have one main power that is dominate in their family. You need to find out what that is."

"I guess I really need to have a long conversation with my mother. Why would she never have even spoke of this type of a talent?" Morgan placed the book near her purse and lifted her wine glass to her lips. She emptied the contents.

"Morgan, now I want you to imagine the wine bottle floating over to you and refilling your glass," Suzy instructed. "Glance at the bottle, concentrate, and in your mind, see the bottle moving according to your wishes."

The baby witch glanced around the circle of other witches, as though looking for approval, and Kinsley was the last one she looked at. She nodded for Morgan to continue.

Morgan took in a deep breath, held out her glass as she stared at the bottle. Again, on command, the wine bottle floated up, over to Morgan and tipped until wine poured in and then returned to the table. Her lips rounded as she gasped at her own talents. She met

Kinsley's gaze. "Is that all this takes? Just envisioning something to happen?"

Angela chimed in. "Yes, it is. Looked what you've learned in a short time."

"But aren't there spells and chanting to make magick happen?"

"Not always. There are certain spells required to create a ward of protection, for example. Those spells are found in your family grimoire, but you need to be able to ask your mother about the book." Kinsley so wanted to take this woman under her wing, but Suzy seemed to have done that, so she would let Suzy continue.

"As a matter of fact, I did call my mother, and we had a long conversation. She is bringing me the grimoire next week and will be staying for a few days."

Morgan looked as though she were worried about getting the information she wanted. Disappointment spread over her face. Kinsley felt bad for her, but wanted to be sure her coven was well trained in case another situation came up with the California coven again. "Another thing we all need to know is how to defend ourselves should we be attacked by others, be it another shifter group, or another coven who wants to take control of our community. I won't allow that to happen. We must continue to practice our self-defense with each other, so we are ready. Rafe said some of the shifters would be willing to show us more moves to become better."

Suzy agreed. "Jake said we should meet at the gym and work out there."

"I agree. Saturday is open for me. I can be away from the cabins for a while," Jenna said.

Kinsley made a note in her phone, as did the others and after another thirty minutes of helping Morgan learn a few more things, the coven members went home. She wanted to talk a few things over with Rafe so things would be ready for next Saturday at the gym.

Chapter 6

Nate rode along with Rafe for the twenty minutes it took to reach Hag Stone so they could speak with Diablo. He wanted to hear the bartender's point of view. Rafe hoped Kinsley's coven meeting went smoothly and that no additional issues came up. He looked forward to her spending the weekend at his place so they could have some alone time free of outside problems. The fact that she refused to commit to moving in with him was like a bur in his side, but he understood a broken heart and the fear of opening up again, even though he didn't like it. The memory of holding her close and breathing in her vanilla scent always made him hard, and thinking about this right now just made the ride more uncomfortable.

Their relationship was anything but normal. He knew neither of them had found their true mate yet, if it could be compared to the crazy mating ritual shifters experienced. His feelings for Kinsley were strong, but he couldn't honestly say he'd claimed her. Sex was great but as a mate, their sex wasn't frenzied like he'd seen others go through. Did that mean their relationship would never go anywhere? He wasn't sure at all, nor did he want to consider a future without her at this point.

Tonight, his wolf needed to run the woods and get rid of pent-up anxiety at the murders in his county and his relationship at the same time. This had to stop, and his shifters were working hard with patrols to keep them safe. Yet, whoever or whatever this was that killed those in his community, it needed to be stopped now.

Rafe yanked open the door of the *Dragon's Lair* with more force than intended, followed by Nate, who always had his back. He had already sensed that other pack members were inside who were enemies, and his mood would make it easy to start a fight. His sense of smell went on high alert and his wolf clawed to be free. He met the gazes of a few rough looking bikers near the door.

Most refused to meet his gaze, knowing who he was, but one insisted on challenging him and stood up. Definitely not one of *his* pack members so where did he come from? Rafe stopped in his tracks and set his shoulders as he lifted his chin in a solid stance, staring at his shorter challenger until he nodded, looked away and sat back down.

Rafe clenched his jaw. "Good choice, son. Don't let me catch you on the wrong side of the law." He glanced over his shoulder to be sure Nate wouldn't fly off the handle. He was always looking out for Rafe and did much of the clean-up when necessary. They made their way to the far side of the bar, met by Diablo.

Diablo set an iced cola on the counter over at the side for Rafe and water for Nate. "Those challenges have to get old, boss."

Shaking his head, Rafe sat on a bar stool at the end of the bar, never with his back to the door, and leaned on the bar. "What's the word among your shifters? I don't want them so on edge that they're attack-happy and get injured out there." Diablo was from Mexico, stood a healthy, bearded, 6'5" and covered in tats...dragons on one arm and shoulder, and a skeleton biker on the other. Not many stood in his way. He was a grizzly shifter, so normally no one threatened him.

He ran a wet bar towel over the counter, his black tee shirt form-fitting his arms and chest. "Most of them have more anger than anything. Just the thought of someone around here killing a tourist, but then gutting them to lay alone and cold in the woods, or on the beach, is a bit sick. One of my guys found the body here in our woods a mile out back."

Diablo met Rafe's gaze and leaned close to whisper. "Billy Joe cleans up around here, and he hasn't reported for work in two days. Although he's not the sharpest tack in the box, and moves at his own speed, he shows up to do his job. But not these last two days. I'm a little worried. He'd be an easy target, Rafe. My guys are searching in four-hour shifts. The next group is due back in an hour."

Nate nodded. "Rafe and I want on the next shift. This bastard has to be stopped."

"They leave their clothes piled a half mile out at the forked trail. We can meet up and change out." Diablo refilled Rafe's cola and began beer refills for the other table.

"Who's tending bar while you're out with us?" Rafe drew his brows together, hoping it wouldn't be a mortal.

"Stephanie will be here in twenty minutes. She's volunteered to go out, but I haven't put her on patrol yet. Not that she couldn't rip that killer to pieces if she came up on him! I know she'd enjoy that too much!" Diablo tipped his head back and let out howling laugh.

The shifters at the front table had a few more join them, male and female, and they took over two more tables that they pulled close together. The noise levels went up several decibels. The beer flowed fast and furiously.

Nate caught Diablo's gaze and nodded toward the bikers. "Stephanie gonna be able to handle them with us gone?"

Again, the muscled bartender laughed. "Some of them have seen her in action. They know she won't take any bullshit. At least I brought an equal partner up here with me. We both love the states, and we know our crowds. Better than that...they know us and our take-no-shit attitudes if they want a fun place to gather."

The bell on the door chimed and all three men looked toward the thick door. Rafe instantly took in Stephanie's appearance as she strode in wearing her tight-ass jeans, biker boots, black tank top, leather vest, and carried in her helmet. She stood taller than the average woman and had a muscular build, definitely a woman who could take care of herself. The guys at the tables cheered with wolf-whistles that she came on duty and shouted for more beer. She passed out a few hugs and checked their glasses.

With a huge smile on her face, she strode toward Rafe, arms stretched out to give him a bear hug. "Hey, Sheriff, you sexy hunk of a man. Good to see you. Nate, same." She stepped over to give him a hug, too.

"Stop with the face sucking, we got work to do, woman!" Diablo teased her.

She pointed a manicured thumb in her partner's direction but whispered to Rafe. "Let me know when I get to run wild and free with your sexy wolf side, Sheriff."

Rafe chuckled. "I ain't touching that with a ten-foot pole, dear! Though I have no doubt it would be wild with a beauty like you!" He winked at Diablo to make sure he knew it was just a tease, and Diablo was already laughing.

Nate stood, finished his water, and headed to the men's room.

Rafe pushed back his empty glass. "We'll meet you out back so we can catch up with the guys and run." Running wild in the woods to let his wolf have free rein helped keep the craving down, but with so much anxiety accumulating from the murders, would it be possible to accomplish?

Ten minutes later, the three of them hurried toward the forked path where the other patrol was just getting back. Diablo spoke with them before they strode back toward the Dragon's Lair. As he pulled off his vest and tee shirt, exposing all his tats, Rafe met his dark gaze. "They said all appeared quiet, but they had the early patrol. Let's hope our watch is uneventful."

Rafe's insides felt clawed as his impatient wolf wanted loose. He stripped off his uniform, and along with the other two, ran off down the path, shifting as his steps turned in leaps. Free at last, he let his spirit animal take over, suddenly smelling everything woodsy. Forever on the alert when he prowled and patrolled, his sense of smell was the first thing that alerted him to danger. Tonight, he hoped all would be fine as they split up, yet within range of each other.

They'd been running for an hour in the forest, in one direction, toward the ocean, when Rafe caught the scent. His gut knotted at the smell of old blood mixed with the salty ocean breeze. He stopped to listen. Nate or Diablo would howl if they found something. Crows cawed overhead as they circled. That only meant one thing.

Rafe followed the scent, praying it wouldn't be Billy Joe. He didn't deserve to die. None of them did, for that matter.

The smell of blood stopped Rafe as he peered down a ravine. He leapt down into the underbrush, then pushed the ground cover with his claws, searching under ferns and old log piles. A booted foot appeared under some leaves, and he stepped back. He couldn't see yet if it was male or female, but he howled for backup and waited until the other two arrived before he dug further.

Nate and Diablo came crashing down into the ravine through the brush and Rafe shifted back as they approached, both doing the same. "We've got a body here."

"I smell it." Diablo shook off the last of his shift and stepped forward to push the pile of leaves out of the way. "Son of a bitch! I'll kill the bastard myself when I find him."

Rafe stepped over and saw the body of Billy Joe, hair, or fur, on the back of his fingers and thick hair halfway up his arms, but the rest of his body looked human...except for his guts. He was sliced from sternum to pelvis, his skin caved in from lack of internal organs.

Something was different about this killing.

It was messy.

The incision appeared precise, but internal organs were strewn about the body, yet the kidneys and heart were missing.

"We can't take him back like this. It ain't right." Diablo ran both hands down his face and over his beard.

"I have to report this, man. I'm sorry. He didn't deserve this. I'm just glad he hadn't fully shifted. That would raise too many questions." Thoughts flew through Rafe's mind. He didn't want to call in back-up, but his position might not give him a choice. If they couldn't find a suspect or some leads soon, he'd have to call in a special investigator.

Along with Nate, they scoured the area for any clues but again, found nothing. Whoever the guilty party was, they knew not to leave evidence.

"Let's get him back to the path and I'll call the coroner to meet us back behind the bar." Nate brushed off the remaining leaves and together they carried Billy Joe back to where their clothes were.

Once dressed, Rafe made notes in his pad and put it back in his pocket. "This wasn't done today or even yesterday. I just don't get it. Who the hell would do this? What's happening with the damn body parts?"

Diablo shuffled as they waited for the coroner. "I hate to even say this, but...organ harvesting happens too often down in Mexico. Big money can be made from those who need healthy parts. The butchers who do this don't give a shit, and they don't have a soul. Money talks and it's all that matters. That's who we're looking for."

"I've never heard of this happening here in the states, and certainly not this far north. This isn't just males because the body the other day was female that Bryce brought in. The coroner isn't going to like having another body in his morgue. I doubt he's been this busy in years. Maybe he's heard from other doctors about transplants. I'm not sure they even discuss this type of thing." Rafe rubbed the back of his neck. The muscles knotted out of control. He'd never seen this many bodies in this condition let alone three in a row. He'd make a few phone calls tomorrow.

"It's a thing, believe me, boss. I got too close when I lived down there." Diablo turned his back on his employee's body. "I hate that seeing him like this is how I will remember him."

Rafe gripped Diablo's shoulder. "Sorry, man. I was hoping he would just walk through your front door and not be found out here."

The coroner met them out back and Rafe noticed that he watched each of them closely. He seemed a bit nervous as he used a pencil to move flesh out of his way to see inside. Rafe noticed that he gave him a side eye then went back to covering the body and he wondered about the coroner being so nervous. That wasn't like him at all.

An hour later, the body on its way to the morgue, Rafe and Nate headed back to Pebble Cove. They'd been gone for three hours, and the dark drive back was quiet. If he and Nate didn't figure out something soon and find some evidence, the State would be crawling all over these towns. He didn't want that. The publicity wasn't the type he wanted to be known for. The tourists would flock here for the wrong reasons, along with the press.

Rafe dropped Nate at the station and checked his phone before he headed home. There was a missed call from Kinsley thirty minutes ago. He hit her speed dial and waited.

"Hi, babe. How was Diablo?"

He had to tell her, but not over the phone. "He said to tell you hi. You and Angela alone?"

"We are. You need another drink?"

Her voice calmed him more than any drink would. "I need *something*. I'll be out in ten minutes."

The yard lights lit up as he walked toward Kinsley's back door. Rafe surveyed the area around the old Victorian before he knocked, needing to be sure nothing was amiss out by the trees. Safety was his main thought where Kinsley was concerned. They never identified the shifters who had trespassed and no one in his pack had heard anything from the neighboring packs.

Kinsley opened the door before he knocked. He took in her vision from head to toe, then wrapped his arms around her, carrying her as he stepped inside. Her warmth surrounded him after running through the woods and dealing with yet another death. Rafe squeezed her tight and just stood there, taking in her comfort.

She nuzzled his neck and kissed his skin with her warm lips. "Hey...you've been out running. Whatever has happened, we can talk about it."

Regretfully, he let go of her and held her at arm's length. Her eyes held understanding, and he knew they could discuss anything. Although...he knew he shouldn't be talking about a murder case with anyone outside of the station. "Jack on the rocks. Make it double."

"You got it." Kinsley walked him into the dining room where their liquor was. She filled his glass with ice and poured the bourbon over it. "Angela went upstairs for the night to give us some privacy."

Before Rafe took his glass from the counter, he took Kinsley's face in his hands and kissed her gently at first. This wasn't the way he wanted to start out, but he needed to feel her. He needed to feel her warmth and taste her. She responded with equal heat, wrapping her arms around his neck. She tasted of whiskey already and he sucked it in, devouring her mouth. His arms went around her body, never wanting to let her go. She could make him forget everything so easily. Slowly, reluctantly, he released her and kissed her forehead. "I'm just glad you're safe."

She took in a deep breath as her fingers trailed over his face. Her green eyes held his for a moment before she spoke. "I better pour *myself* a double. Then let's go sit in the living room."

Rafe turned on a small lamp in the living room and sat on the sofa. He pulled Kinsley close as she sat down, and he explained what had happened on their patrol in Hag Stone. By the time he finished, so was his drink.

"I'll get you another. That's just too much shit to deal with. I'm sorry, babe." When she returned, he took another long drink. "What is your next step in the investigations? This is demented, and we have a killer on the loose here."

"I'm hoping the coroner has some evidence for us on this one since Nate and I didn't find a shred of it on the scene. Billy Joe didn't deserve that. Diablo said organ harvesting runs heavily down south below the border. Big business, big money. I'm going to do some digging to see if I can find something on any cases down there." He swirled the ice in his glass. "I can't even imagine the type of person it takes to pull this shit off."

"Someone is making money off the organs that are removed from these bodies?" Kinsley's warm fingers rested on his thigh, her nails gently scraping his pants as she did so.

"Yes. There must be something we're not seeing. This person has to get the organs to their buyer within a certain number of hours after removal, so they have to be using helicopters or boats for the quickest way out of here to a hospital. I'm baffled. This is so far out of the ordinary. My God, what a sick mind to pull this off. I also asked the coroner to keep quiet on Bobby Joe's murder if he could. We don't need a shifter body under the microscope."

Kinsley lifted her head from his shoulder. "Would this be something Destiny might run across in the tissue samples she gets?"

He stared at her. Just the mention of Destiny's name made his pulse race. Whatever it was between them, it made him think twice. He wasn't sure if she felt it, too, but it was real, and he couldn't ignore it. What would happen if she came back to town and offered to help? Yet he needed to speak with her. "Shit! I've never thought of that. I should give her a call to see if she might know anything about where the tissue samples come from when she receives them."

Grabbing her phone, she texted Destiny's number to him. "There. You can call her when you're ready."

Gibbs came racing into the living room and up on to Kinsley's lap. He stretched across her legs and put one paw on Rafe's thigh as he tipped his head to the side as he looked up at Rafe.

He was awarded with Rafe giving him pets on the top of his head. "Were you feeling left out? We didn't mean to do that."

Kinsley laughed and stroked Gibbs' fur, tussling him around to pick him up and hug her familiar. "You are just so cute, buddy."

Gibbs looked over at Rafe, and he could have sworn that the ferret stuck out his tongue at him! "I won't get between you and your mommy, Mr. Gibbs. I promise."

* * * * *

After leaving the station, Nate put his car into drive just as his phone rang. He put it back into park when he recognized the number, but it was too late for Morgan to be calling. What the hell?

"Nate, I just got home from Kinsley's and the front door to my shop has busted glass and the door is wide open. I'm in my car with the doors locked behind the store." Morgan's voice cracked as she talked.

"I'll be right there. I was just leaving the station. Don't move." Nate spun out of the parking lot and drove through town until he saw Morgan's car in at the back entrance of her store. He parked behind her and rushed to her driver's window. She rolled it down. "Stay right there until I get back. Give me the key to the back door. Once I make sure it's cleared inside, I'll come back for you. Keep these doors locked until I come back."

With Morgan's key, he opened the door. His shifter sense had already taken over as he shined his flashlight around, his revolver in his other hand. The back of the store appeared untouched, the cash drawer was opened and empty, the way Morgan always left it, to be safe, but the shelving at the front was knocked over and the glass items were broken, as well as the glass in the front door. He listened to be sure no one was hiding, then continued to search the small store. All was clear. Damned kids who vandalized just for the hell of it. What a mess.

He made his way back to Morgan and brought her back inside the store with him, then turned on the lights. With his arm around her, Nate kept his hand on her shoulder for support as she glanced around.

"Why would someone want to destroy my dream of having a bookstore?" Tears welled in her eyes as she turned toward him. He held her tight as her shoulders shook and it was then that he noticed her scent of strawberries. So sweet and soothing and his wolf took notice. His heart race with a need he'd never experienced before, and his inner animal wanted to take over. This had to be his mate but now was not the proper time, and he kept his claws down.

Chapter 7

Morgan leaned away from Nate and again, stared at the devastation. "If I didn't know better, I would think my ex destroyed this like he did all of my other dreams."

"Do you seriously think he would do this? I need to know. Is he in town?"

"Not that I know of, but I haven't been watching for him. How am I ever going to get this cleaned up? I hate this and I hate him!" Morgan wiped at her tears as she walked toward the damage. "I wish I could just swirl my fingers, and it would all be back the way it was!" With a whirl of her hand, she wished it so. Miraculously, before her eyes, pieces of glass came together in the door, and the shelving righted itself. The broken ornaments and figurines put themselves back together where she'd had them on the shelves. "Oh, my goddess, Nate!"

She turned toward him as his eyes widened. He couldn't believe what he'd just witnessed. Had he not seen it for himself, he would not have believed it possible.

"Morgan…what just happened?" Did this woman before him possess magick like Kinsley and her coven?

Morgan had turned back toward the front door, now repaired like nothing had happened. Then she faced Nate again. "I'm in shock, I'm sure. Tell me you saw the broken glass everywhere!"

"It was. We both saw it. But…" He had no more words. He'd seen her swirl her hand and the next he saw the glass find its way back into place as if nothing had happened. This wasn't his first time being around magick since Kinsley was a witch, as was Suzy.

Nate walked over to the door to make sure it was locked and secure, then glanced at the floor. No broken glass anywhere. The shelving now held each item as it had before, nothing broken, but all mended. He looked back at Morgan.

She rubbed her hands together and shook them out. "Kinsley said all I needed to do was envision what I want and with a whirl of my fingers, things would happen. Never, ever did I think magick would fix a mess like that. I still don't understand." She stared at Nate and shook her finger. "No one can know this happened until I understand it myself. Promise me, Nate." Again, tears pooled in her blues eyes.

Nate stepped over to wrap her in his arms. "It's our secret. Until we know exactly what happened. Obviously, you have abilities like Kinsley. It's ok, hon. But at some point, I need to let Rafe know that a break-in happened." She trembled in his arms.

First, her store is broken and destroyed, then she finds out she has magickal abilities. How could he help her? Nate took her face in his hands and connected their gazes. Her blue eyes pooled with tears and tugged at his heart. "Hey, it's going to be okay. I want to make sure you get upstairs and that your apartment is untouched."

"Okay. We can lock the back door on our way up." She looked around again. "I can't believe what just happened."

Nate met her gaze. Her white complexion and wide eyes told him that he needed to get her upstairs before she collapsed. The need to protect her from whoever had done the damage to the store arose strong, and he needed to be there for her. Finding the suspect wouldn't be easy since he found no clues left in the area.

Leading her toward the thick, heavy back door, Nate locked it and gave her the keys back. Morgan had started up, and he followed her, his hearing on high alert for any sound of intruders. The damage didn't appear that anyone had made it to the back of the store, but he wanted to be ready.

All appeared to look normal. No damage had come this far. She unlocked the door, and he followed her into the small apartment. One small lamp by the sofa gave a soft light to the tiny living room, and Morgan turned on more lights. After setting her purse and keys on the table, her hands began to shake.

Late onset of shock. Nate knew what it was. He took her by the arm and led her toward the sofa to sit. "Can I get you a drink? I think you could use one."

"There is wine on the counter and beer in the fridge. Help yourself, Nate. Glasses are in the top cabinet." Her shaky voice sounded like a whisper. Nate pulled down a glass and half filled it with wine, though he thought something stronger would be better for her.

He grabbed a beer and joined her on the sofa. With trembling fingers, Morgan placed both hands around the glass and took a long pull of the wine. As he watched her pale lips touch the rim of the glass, Nate thought about how soft they'd be against his own. How long had she been single? Had her ex abused her? He wanted to know more about Morgan's past. That information might help him search for a suspect.

She took another sip and sat back against the sofa, cupping the glass in her fingers. Fingers he'd love to feel on his face or shoulder. Morgan looked thin and frail at the moment. The frightening break-in had taken a toll on her tonight. There was no way she should be alone right now, and he hadn't had any plans.

Nate sat close and put his arm around her shoulder. Thankfully, she cuddled into his embrace but felt no warmth coming from her. He set his beer on the coffee table and pulled down the afghan behind them to cover her lap. She took the edge in her small fingers to pull it up higher under her arms. He grabbed his beer again and settled her close beneath his arm.

When her blue eyes met his gaze, he saw emptiness and it tugged at his heart. His inner wolf clawed at him to make a move, but the timing wasn't right. The last thing she needed right now was for him to shock her again. Her eyes searched his. Questions nearly tumbled out at him.

"I can't thank you enough for coming here tonight. I didn't know who else to call this late."

"I'm glad you did. I was just leaving the station. Rafe and I were over in Hag Stone talking with Diablo and Stephanie. They're all concerned about the murders, and when I saw your name appear on my phone, I can honestly say it scared me. I'm glad you are alright, and the damage was minimal." There was no way he could mention they'd found Bobby Joe's body. She likely didn't know him, but neither did she need to hear that tonight.

"I didn't want to call my son and scare him. He doesn't need to know this happened."

"You have a son in town?" Nate would file that information.

"Yes, Logan graduated college and moved here with me so we could both make a new start after my divorce. I've been divorced for five years. Getting him through college was not easy as a single mom. His father is an asshole. I don't know how I stayed with him as long as I did." She emptied her wine. "Cheers to being away from him."

Nate now knew she had no protector besides her son, and perhaps he couldn't even protect his mother. He hoped he would get a chance to see what type of man he was. "What does Logan do here?"

"He has his own apartment and fills in at the coffee shop for me. The customers love his specialty drinks he makes for them. He's even created a list of several different coffees for them to taste." Morgan rolled her empty glass in her hands.

"Would you like more wine? It seems to have helped calm you down some." Nate wanted to learn more about Morgan and didn't want to leave just yet.

"I don't want to take up your entire evening." Her eyes pleaded with him to stay, and he couldn't resist her need.

"I didn't have any plans for tonight, so no worries. But I don't want to overstay and make you uncomfortable."

"Strange. I don't feel uncomfortable here with you at all. You're easy to be with. You give off comforting vibes. I like that." She held up her glass. "Please get another beer if you like."

Morgan's fingers touched Nate's as he took the glass from her, and she felt stabs of electricity travel up her arm. Immediately, she looked up at him. He paused a moment, allowing their fingers to stay connected and she could see that he felt it, too.

The color of his eyes deepened as he smiled. "I'll get us both a refill."

As she waited, she glanced around her small living room for any signs of Izzy. Strange that she couldn't feel the old woman at all. Perhaps she knew Morgan was not in a threatening situation and her nerves were calming. She still couldn't believe that the glass and damage was repaired with a swirl of her fingers. The coven needed to know what had happened, but that could wait until tomorrow.

Nate returned and handed her the glass. When he sat down, she leaned forward a bit so he could put his arm over her shoulder again, which he did. She leaned into him, adjusted the afghan, and glanced up at him. His lips were so close, his eyes still darker than normal, and his tongue moistened his parted lips. All she had to do was lean closer, but was she ready for that? The two of them hadn't even spent time together before tonight, yet it felt as though they'd known each other for years. *How could this be?*

Her ex-husband had never un-nerved her like this, nor made her insides flip over like butterflies. So why had she married him and stayed so long? *Her son.* That was why. Did she ever truly love her husband? Because what she felt at this moment seemed new. As though she were sixteen again.

When warm lips touched hers, she didn't back away but closed her eyes. Then pressure opened her own lips as his tongue moved over her lower lip. The sensation sent sparks through her entire body. The kiss didn't last long and when Nate pulled back, his forehead rested on hers.

"I shouldn't have done that, but I won't apologize. I've wanted to do that since the day I saw you at Suzy's shop." Nate sat as still as a statue.

Morgan moved away first, but not far. She looked into those sexy eyes of his, and her core heated. *This is insane!* She doesn't even know Nate, yet…those feelings were there that she'd never felt for anyone before. Like a crazy teenager not knowing when it was time to stop, she leaned forward and pressed her lips to his again. Nate reached over to set down his beer, and his fingers curved behind her neck to thread through her hair. His tongue touched hers like fire to a torch. Careful with her glass, her other fingers went behind Nate's neck and pulled him closer.

A slight moan slipped from her throat, sending a small shock wave up her back, tingling toward his fingers in her hair. Embarrassed, Morgan leaned out from the kiss and stared at Nate. "I don't know what came over me. I don't want you to think I kiss every man I meet. This never happens, Nate."

Nate's thumb crooked beneath her chin and lifted her face. "Don't apologize. Don't ruin what just happened. This was special. Not something I do either. I've been single a long time because I haven't met the right woman yet." The pad of his thumb moved over her lower lip as she met his gaze.

His touch had ignited a fire within her center, and she couldn't contain it. "One step at a time. Tonight, hasn't been a normal evening. The break in. Me repairing it all with a whirl of my hand. I'm still in shock over that more than the break-in. I'll have to talk with Suzy about this tomorrow for sure." Morgan took a drink of her wine, and Nate retrieved his beer and took a long pull, then sat back.

For several minutes, they sat silent as she tried to make sense of her feelings that Nate had started. Moving to Pebble Cove seemed to have changed many things for her.

Nate leaned close. "It's not too late. Would you like to go over to Krazy Local's for a quick bite to eat? They serve a mean burger and fries."

What would it hurt? She hadn't eaten this afternoon, and her stomach let her know that.

"Let me go freshen up after that scare. At least I don't feel so shaken up." In the bathroom, Morgan ran a brush though her hair, seeing her reddened lips in the mirror. Her fingers moved over her lips, remembering Nate's kisses. *Goddess, it felt good.* A dinner out to get her mind off of everything would be just the magick she needed.

Two hours later, Morgan leaned her shoulders against the heavy back door where Nate had just left. During dinner, they talked about their pasts, their likes and dislikes. It had turned out to be a good evening despite what had brought them together. She trudged up the stairs, wishing Nate had come up with her. Once inside, she turned the deadbolt on her door. After she hung up her sweater, she easily sensed a ripple that went through the air.

Morgan glanced at the overstuffed armchair where Izzy had made herself comfortable. "How long have you been here?"

"I'm usually here even when you can't see me. I hope you realize that I gave you privacy when that handsome young man came up here to make sure everything was okay. You might want to refill that wine glass. We need to have a chat, my dear."

Morgan stared at her momentarily, until Izzy waved her on toward the kitchen. Confused, she poured until her glass was full this time and returned to sit on the sofa. "So, you are aware of what happened downstairs tonight?"

"Of course, I am. I might be old, but I don't miss much. And I know *who* did it, just not why it was done." Izzy laced her gnarled fingers together and rested them in her lap. "Does your ex-husband still want you back?"

Blinking, as if that would clear her head, Morgan glared at Izzy. "That's a moot point. I would never go back to him. It's been a long five years since our divorce. Yes, he was angry when I left with my son. He's always been angry about that, but Logan didn't want to live with his father and that was his choice." She tipped her head to reconsider. "What does my ex have to do with the break-in?"

"He used a sledgehammer to break the glass, came in and tipped over a few display shelves and left laughing. No one saw him when he left so I doubt he will ever be connected to this unless you make a phone call to him. But congratulations on cleaning up the mess so quickly. I knew you had it in you the day you came into my store."

"Can witches sense other witches? If so, why can't I sense it?" She didn't remember noticing anything strange the day she met Suzy or Kinsley, other than a slight tingle when they touched. Nor did she sense anything when she met Izzy and bought the store.

"It will get easier the more you learn. When your mother arrives next week, she will reveal much to you, just be prepared."

Morgan straightened her head as she gritted her teeth. Damn her mother anyway. "I'll certainly have a list of questions I want answered, beginning with why she thought I didn't need to know about this shit. This is more than frustrating. She better have a damn good reason why. My childhood and teen years could have been a lot easier had I known I could make my own life easier. I would have started with *not* getting married!"

Izzy watched her with her soft eyes. "I'm sure she thought her reasoning was right at the time. You also have a psychic ability, but when it concerns your personal life, you won't be able to see things coming."

Being able to have that ability when she was younger could have helped her in many ways. Life could have made way more sense, but rather, her mother had chosen to let her flounder on her own. *Why?* That just didn't make sense to her.

The wine tannins hit her tongue before the soothing flavor. Perhaps she should have poured whiskey instead! She took another drink anyway.

Another sip, then another.

Morgan couldn't wait until her mother showed up. As she swirled the wine in her glass, she envisioned different times in her childhood when her mother had acted strange and now things were making more sense. "She better bring her spell book and all my answers."

"It's called a family grimoire. All will be better once she explains the ways of our world. There is much that is complicated. It's not just casting spells and having things repaired with the swirl of your hand. There is the Witch's Council, which may be restricting what your mother could reveal to you and when."

She blinked as if to clear her mind, not truly understanding the ramifications of what Izzy had just told her and set her hand and glass on the arm of the sofa. Thoughts were like a tornado in Morgan's head trying to understand why her mother would let her live without understanding what all of this means. *Why does this all sound so foreign?* "What the hell is this Witch's Council?"

Izzy cast her gaze down to her hands and took a deep breath. Several moments passed, and Morgan waited for her to contemplate an explanation. How difficult could the answer be? And why would this *council* have anything to do with her mother? Or her? She kept her attention on Izzy, not wanting to rush an answer, but she needed to know so much.

When Izzy looked at Morgan, her eyes seemed darker and eerie. Her clasped fingers tightened and released several times. "The Witch's Council are basically the judges and prosecutors over the witch and warlock community. Laws are in place that guide every coven. One major law is to never kill another witch or warlock, ever. The council deals with those responsible. They are usually elders of the community, meaning some could be hundreds of years old. I was never on the council, but...I was nearly two hundred years old when I passed." A tear slipped down her cheek.

Morgan pressed her other hand over her heart and gasped. "Oh, my goddess, Izzy. I had no idea."

"That, also, is your mother's fault. I'll be here when she arrives even though I won't be seen unless you call on me. She may feel my presence, and I'll try to shield myself from her, but I'm not sure how strong her powers are. Even now, all you have to do is summon me in your mind, and I will be able to hear your requests for help."

"Surely you are more powerful than my mother!"

"I will know more once she arrives." Izzy slowly rose from her seat, patted Morgan's hand, shuffled toward the back of the apartment, and disappeared.

Darkness seemed to envelope Morgan even though the lights were on. Loneliness took over her heart now. She wondered what the reason could be that her mother refused to teach her of her abilities or what her future might be like. There were so many questions and no answers. She really had no one to turn to except her new friends, and they alone had started to teach her. For that, Morgan would always be grateful.

A yawn escaped when she realized how late it was. So much had happened today, and exhaustion took over. Her brain was overloaded rather than being calm. After finishing her wine, she dropped into bed, hopefully to forget and rest. "Good night, Izzy...."

Chapter 8

Once again, the internet connection got interrupted, and Kinsley rattled her modem as she gritted her teeth in frustration. After unplugging it, then plugging it back in, like the tech support people constantly told her to do, nothing seemed to work. With her flashlight in hand, she stomped past her receptionist. "I need to go check the wires in the basement...again. This is getting ridiculous. The cable company may have to come back and rewire this place. I'll be back."

As her stiletto heels clicked on the old marble hallway floor, Kinsley strode toward the basement door. *Damn technology anyway. This building needed to be upgraded.* Unlatching the chain that blocked the stairway, she flipped the switch, and carefully took each step to the bottom. The musty odor sent her hand to cover her nose. "I hate it down here. Whoever is listening, stop fucking with the internet!"

She clicked on the flashlight and shined it on the electrical panel across the damp basement when a cold ripple of air passed her, sending an icy cold chill over her skin.

The lights flickered twice.

Then the lights went black.

Kinsley held up her hand. "Okay! I'm sorry!"

As if by her own magick, the lights relit the basement. She swiped at the cobwebs, flipped a switch and swore under her breath again.

A stone hit her in the back as she walked toward the panel, and she spun around, blue electricity sparking from her fingers. The dark apparition sent her back a step or two as she widened her eyes to be sure of what she saw.

A huge, hooded figure stood before her, and she could feel the emanating power. She calmed the sparks from her fingers. "What do you want?"

"You know why I'm here again?" The deepness of his voice tugged at her senses of danger being nearby.

"I have no idea. I've already satisfied your demands." Kinsley remembered what had happened when the California coven visited last year. Two of their witches had been gravely wounded and close to death because of her powers. "Those two still live. You should not be concerned with them now."

Harsh breathing came with a foul odor. "You have a powerful witch in your community, and I want her. She is to be dealt with before more trouble is started. She has powers that cause us issues."

Kinsley slowly stepped toward the stairs as she replied, hoping she could get away. "I have no idea who that might be. Why does it concern me? How am I supposed to stop her when I don't know who she is?"

"You'll know soon enough. I'll be in touch, my dear." With that, the apparition disappeared.

Kinsley hurried over to the steps, grabbed the handrail, and took a few deep breaths as she looked behind her to be sure that thing was gone. As High Priestess of her coven, she had made a deal with the dark side to rid their community of the California coven. She knew better at the time. Now she needed to let Angela know he was back.

Damn it.

She wondered if Angela would know who this witch was in Pebble Cove. Now her mind wouldn't rest until she knew, and her reports needed to be done today. *Good luck concentrating on that!*

By the time she got back to her office, the receptionist was working again. "Whatever you did down there worked! I hope you didn't make a deal with the devil!"

Kinsley just rolled her eyes on her way back to her office. "You have no idea!" Relieved that the internet connected, she sat down to gather her thoughts. Being downstairs spooked her out. She hated that basement, and for good reason.

Her phone messenger buzzed. Suzy requested a call back. Kinsley dialed her number.

"Are you alone right now?" The urgency in Suzy's voice made the hairs on her neck stand up.

"I am. What's up? This isn't like you."

"Morgan just left my shop. She said her mother is making a visit in a few days and is bringing items that pertain to her abilities. Her mother said she was glad she would be able to get Morgan up to speed, but the information would have to wait until she got here. She also told me that her store was broken into last night and that Nate came to help her check things out. He didn't find anyone on the premises, but Morgan had envisioned her damaged shop being back to normal and suddenly, the broken glass from the door floated back into place and the tipped over shelving righted itself. She was pretty shaken up over the fact that she could even do that. Morgan has no idea what all of her powers entail so it should be interesting when her mom arrives."

"Oh, my goddess. Does she need us to go over there?" Kinsley tapped a pen on her desk. The demon had told her someone with powerful abilities was in town. This could all be very interesting.

"No, she wants to keep it hush-hush until she speaks with her mom. I'd certainly like to meet that woman!"

"Perhaps she'll give us that opportunity. We can only hope." Kinsley paused. "Suzy, I just had a visit from the demon when I was in the basement. He's back."

"Shit. We should have known this would happen sooner or later."

"He wants this witch. What if it's Morgan or her mom?"

"Well, that's an issue. We'll have to wait until we hear more from Morgan."

"Let me know if she calls you again. We're here if she needs us." Kinsley disconnected the call and rubbed her temples.

Morgan should not have had to come into her abilities by surprise. Mothers who did this to their children weren't doing them any favors. She wondered how powerful Morgan was since she had no idea. Shielding them from the council was the only reason Kinsley could think of as a reason. That didn't bode well if, in fact, that was her mother's hope.

For that reason, Kinsley was glad she'd never had any children, but now there would be no daughter to take her spot when she passed. Her ex had been a warlock, but he'd gone to the dark side. Totally against what Kinsley was and she filed for divorce and left. Luckily, he'd left her alone. *But what if he has connections with Dantalion?*

* * * * *

Nate ordered a coffee in the café at the bookstore. "You must be Logan. I'm friends with your mom. It's nice to see you helping her out here."

"I enjoy meeting the customers, and it gives me extra money so I can live on my own and not be a thorn in her side. Creating new coffee drinks is fun, and some are best sellers here. Thanks for stopping by Deputy."

Logan's blue eyes smiled back at Nate, just like his mom. Nate walked around the café and bookstore, watching as the customers came and went, looking for anyone suspicious who might have come back to see last night's damage. None seemed to know about it, nor did anyone do a double take toward the door or the shelving that was now upright.

Nate glanced out the window at the same gray truck across the street as when he went in to get coffee. When the driver made eye contact with him, the driver immediately put the vehicle into gear and drove away. Nate rushed out the door and checked the street.

Nothing.

Not a truck in sight.

He tossed his coffee into the nearest trash bin and got into his car, hoping to drive around to find it. The truck couldn't be far. The license plate could be called in to get the driver's info he wanted. Did the driver have anything to do with the break-in? Nate had no idea what Morgan's ex looked like but would check with her. She'd stated that he didn't live in the area though.

Nate drove down several of the main streets, the hotel parking lots, and shopping centers. No gray truck was parked anywhere. It didn't just disappear. He decided to park back near Morgan's store and watch for the driver to return. Twenty minutes later, he decided to drive around back and check the store's rear door. He sat there for a few minutes in frustration. His future mate needed his protection. He would do everything in his power to keep her safe.

No gray pickups drove by.

He didn't get a good look at the driver but if that had been Morgan's ex, Nate had come so close to talking to him. Was he guilty of breaking the window in her door and knocking over the shelves? Without knowing what her ex looked like, he couldn't be sure. He wondered exactly what her ex had done to make her want a divorce. Morgan was beautiful and deserved to be happy. He'd try his best to be the man she needed.

When he saw her come out of the back door alone and head toward her car, Nate's breath caught as a man approached her and grabbed her arm. The stranger immediately let go of her and shook out his hand and arm. Nate knew instantly that her magick had made him let her go.

He was out of his patrol car without thinking about it and rushed over as they started arguing. "Get your hands off of her!"

"This is none of your business, asshole!" The man grabbed her arm again and pulled Morgan away even though she fought him.

He let go of her as quickly as he'd grabbed her and stared at her. "What the hell is wrong with you? That was an electrical shock!"

Morgan stepped back. "Then stop touching me, you bastard!"

"You can leave her alone, or I can arrest you for assault. That'll keep you locked up long enough to figure this out. So, grab her again, and I'll be tazing you with more electricity than she did!" Nate kept his cool. If he let his wolf out now, it'd create more of a scene. "Your choice, man. Morgan, who is this man?"

She stared at the man with a curl to her lip. "He's my ex. And he was just leaving. Why are you in town anyway?"

Without a word, her ex walked into a nearby alley, got into his truck and pulled away, but not before Nate got his plate number. He quickly jotted it down in his pad and slipped it back in his pocket. Morgan watched him drive away, too. "Sorry you had to deal with him, Morgan."

"I don't know how he found out where I live. I've tried to be very careful. What does he want now? I'll have to check with Logan to see if he's talked with his father." She rubbed her arm. "I don't want to live in fear of him poking around my business, but he received quite an electrical shock when he grabbed me."

"We can keep an eye on his vehicle to make sure he doesn't hang around. Let's get you back inside. Are you sure you're okay?" Nate would rather have raced after the truck to talk to him, but Morgan's safety came first.

"I'm fine. I think I need the safety class Kinsley wants us to attend at the gym. That's a great idea, now that I might have to deal with him again."

* * * * *

Saturday morning, Kinsley got to the gym early, with Rafe, to be sure the area was set up for the women to learn hand to hand combat should they need to defend themselves. She looked forward to the workout.

Last night, she and Rafe had spent the night at her place. Too much alcohol and stress led them up to her bedroom. She shook her head. They certainly had relieved whatever built up energy they both had. Her body still tingled from the touch of his magic fingers...and lips.

Rafe walked over to be sure enough mats were out. As she watched him move, memories of those muscled arms holding her last night made her smile and want him again tonight. Their life was perfect for them, even though she knew he wanted a commitment, but he would never give her an ultimatum. He accepted what she was willing to give for now.

After they'd met, he'd shown her some great protective moves, and it made her more confident knowing she could defend herself if the need arose. Today, her goal was to be sure Morgan could learn some of those same tactics. If her mother couldn't protect her, Kinsley would be sure she did. "Is Nate coming to class today?"

Rafe walked back over to where she stood at the weight bench. His eyes gave her the toe to head once-over, stripping her naked with his eyes, then gave her a sexy smile. "Am I not enough for you today? I was pretty sure I made that clear last night." He took her in his arms.

She ran her fingers over his biceps and body-hugging tee shirt. "You are always enough for me. I was thinking about Morgan. I think she has a thing for Nate. They *are* two lonely people."

"Are you playing matchmaker?" His finger went beneath her chin to raise her face up. His warm lips touched hers, and she kissed him back. "It wouldn't be a bad idea though."

"Her mother hasn't been around for her from what I've gathered. She's supposed to be in town on Sunday. I'd like to meet the woman.

If she has powerful abilities, I'm curious why she didn't train her daughter, so she'd know how to deal with her witch-side." Kinsley's hand rested on the taut muscles over Rafe's chest, and if she didn't step away, they'd be caught in the middle of something neither of them could stop. "I think today will be a good day and a refresher for the others."

Suzy, Jake, and Angela called to them from the door as they dropped their gym bags and joined Kinsley. Rafe let her go, but smacked her ass before she could get away. The heated look he gave her spoke of more fun tonight. She looked forward to some quiet time.

Soon the other girls showed up, and Rafe greeted Nate and Morgan. Kinsley watched them together. They stayed near each other but didn't give any indication they were a couple. Nate was a nice guy and built as powerful as Rafe, in her opinion. The man had never dated anyone that she knew of. He was prior military before joining the force, a loner away from the station, and he was Rafe's right-hand man where the pack was concerned. Nate always had his back. She wondered what type of woman would interest him.

"A penny for your thoughts!" Angela whispered in her ear. "I see you planning something, chickie. That can't be a good thing!" She laughed out loud.

Kinsley turned to laugh with her blue-eyed friend. Angela wore her auburn hair in a ponytail today, too. "Wouldn't they make a good couple? Neither of them is taken yet, so why not? I'm curious to see if anything happens between them. Time will tell." She'd kept her voice low for only Angela to hear.

Rafe had them start out by doing laps around the gym. The women tried to keep up with the guys, but their strides were naturally longer. This made Angela competitive, and she ran ahead of Kinsley as she encouraged Angela not to let the guys win.

When they paired off, Jake partnered with Morgan first to show her a few beginners moves, and Kinsley smiled as she watched how quickly the woman caught on. Jake didn't hold anything back and Morgan held her own against him.

Kinsley paired with Nate. The man knew his own strength and Kinsley wanted all he had. "Don't hold back on my account. I might take you down!"

"And if I hurt you, you know who I answer to!" Nate laughed and allowed himself to be taken down when Kinsley landed her arm across his chest to pull him backward over her leg behind his.

She gazed down at him and took in a deep breath, satisfied with herself. "Then I'll assume you're just a sissy!"

From the mat, Nate swept his arm around her ankles and toppled her, taking her by surprise. She landed next to him. "I know we taught you never to stand so close to your enemy!"

"Touché!" She rolled to her feet, laughing. "You got me on that one. But deep down, I know you're a sweetheart! I won't let that get around though!"

After two hours of training, Kinsley and Rafe met the others at Krazy Locals Restaurant for burgers and beers. She watched Morgan, feeling responsible to keep an eye on her safety until she knew the woman could hold her own. Morgan was in no way a cowering divorcee.

She had confidence as a woman and wanted to be included in the chamber events, so Kinsley would keep that in mind for the planning of the next meeting.

Kinsley felt a ripple in the atmosphere and looked out the windows, then around at the other patrons. A tourist had stepped into the restaurant alone and took a seat in a booth several tables away from them. Her magickal powers were unmistakable, and she looked directly at Morgan...and so did Kinsley. Her protective side took over, and she had to hold back to see how Morgan would handle the silent approach of the stranger.

When Morgan noticed the other woman, all the color in her cheeks disappeared, and her eyes widened. Without a word, Morgan excused herself and approached the stranger, then sat down with her.

Rafe noticed the exchange immediately. "Are you alright? Do you know her?"

"No, but her magick is so strong that I felt it before she came in." Rafe placed his warm hand on Kinsley's thigh for support. She met his eyes. "You felt it too, didn't you?"

He nodded.

She glanced over at Nate and his muscles had taken on a solid impression. He watched Morgan like a guardian, and Kinsley was proud that he cared.

Morgan walked back over to the table to retrieve her purse and drink. "I'm sorry. That woman is my mother. She wasn't supposed to be in town until tomorrow." She looked at Nate. "I'll be fine. I promise. I'll call you later." Morgan left to sit with her mom.

Rafe reached over to touch Nate's arm. "Are *you* alright?"

"I am." Nate turned to Rafe. "I've not told you yet, but her shop had a break-in the other day. She wanted me to keep it quiet, but you need to know. I also saw a strange gray pickup sitting across the street from her store yesterday just watching. When I made eye-contact with him, he took off. I caught up with him around back at her store where he approached Morgan when she walked out the door. I broke it up, and he left, but the store was a mess."

Nate looked at Suzy, then back at Morgan as Suzy spoke up. "I have to tell you that she didn't want you to know. But the broken glass in the door and the shelving that got tipped over shocked her. She had almost no control when suddenly…the broken glass found its way back into the door like it'd never been busted out, and the shelves sat up on their own. She said all broken items were as though they'd never been broken."

Nate shook his head and took a gulp of his beer. "Morgan didn't do anything magickal that I'd seen, but you wouldn't know the break-in had even taken place. She wants to understand how it all happened before she tells you."

Kinsley felt bad for Morgan. "Suzy told me. I hope she can get answers tonight from her mother."

Chapter 9

Morgan slipped into the booth where her mother sat. "Mom...I thought you were going to call so I could meet you at the motel?" Morgan fisted her fingers around the strap of her purse beside her in the seat.

"I didn't know you would be in here. I was going to call you."

"But...you didn't. I hope you didn't drive all day to get here."

"I did. I left San Francisco early this morning. Please don't be mad that I didn't call. I have so much to tell you, but I needed to get a burger first. When we're done here, we'll go back to my room. I think it's better we talk there." Her mom adjusted the amber amulet she always wore around her neck.

Morgan calmed herself, stretched out her fingers and concentrated on drinking the rest of her wine. She glanced outside, unsure of why the atmosphere felt off. Perhaps it was due to her mom's visit, she wasn't sure. Again, angry that she had been kept in the dark for so many years. If she'd been properly trained, she might understand why the world appeared off kilter once in a while.

"You're right. I shouldn't have tried to shield you from the magick. Then you wouldn't have so many questions for me."

Her eyes widened that her mother could read her mind. "Is that an ability I have and don't know it? How much is there to tell me, mom?" Morgan stared into her red wine, and her anger made it swirl like the questions in her head.

Her mom's fingers curled over her wrist. "Please don't do this to yourself. You need to remain as calm as possible, and the wine will stop swirling. I have items in my room that I need to give you, but until then, let's talk about other things. How is the store going? How is Logan doing?"

As soon as her mother touched her wrist, the wine stilled when her anger subsided.

What the hell?

Yet, more unanswered questions.

Her mother's soft voice reached her. "Please don't."

Morgan straightened her back, and her mother's fingers lifted. "Logan helps out at my coffee shop. The customers love him. He creates special coffee drinks for them and enjoys hearing what is happening in their lives. We now have several regulars on a daily basis. Things are going well, mom."

She looked at her mother as though it were the first time, seeing her now as a different person. Her light brown hair was cut short and combed back, the top and bangs teased to a beautiful look, accenting her high cheekbones. Sophisticated. Properly dressed like a businesswoman. Then again, she was. Her mother, Annette Scott, had always worked, owning one of the top jewelry stores in a suburb of San Francisco, so money was never a problem for her. Morgan had never worried that her mother would be out on the street somewhere. Her father had his own business that kept him traveling often, but again, she had no idea exactly what he did.

"It makes me feel better knowing that you both are doing fine."

She wasn't fine, but she refused to discuss what just happened at her store and how shit repaired itself with little effort. And there was no way she was going to let Logan know what had happened.

Finishing her wine as her mother paid her bill, Morgan walked out with her, waving at Nate, and hoping he understood.

Once in her mom's room, Morgan set her purse on the dresser and sat down in the recliner in the small motel room decorated in teals and yellows. On the bed were two boxes that her mother began to open. First, she removed a velvet box and sat on the edge of the bed near Morgan.

She handed her the box. "Before we begin, I need you to put that on and promise you will never take it off."

Her mother's blue eyes begged her to understand and give her time. Morgan opened it, and there on white velvet lay a beautiful amethyst quartz shaped like a half-moon, wrapped with silver wire in the form of the tree of life on a long silver chain.

She looked up at her mother through tears that pooled in her own eyes. "It's beautiful." Morgan carefully removed it from the box and placed it around her neck, then covered it with her fingers. Immediately the jewelry tingled and warmed to her skin.

"It will always protect you and your powers. It will also keep your powers hidden from the demons around you."

"What are you talking about?"

Annette sat up straight and took in a breath. "There are other powers besides ours, my dear. I'm not sure how best to explain it to you, because so much happened so many years ago. It involved my parents and a deal they made with a demon after I was born. This evil person wanted to take me away, and my parents had to flee, hiding me from this demon and all he could do."

She touched her own amber amulet. "This, along with yours, was warded by the Goddess years ago to protect me and my powers from the demon so I couldn't be found or tracked ever again. I bound your powers for as long as I could, but once you turned forty, the magick was out of my control. That's how our family works. My powers were bound, and I found out about it the hard way. The demon discovered me and took me away."

Tears pooled in her mother's eyes and for the first time, Morgan felt sorry for her mother. "I won't go into what I endured. That's not why I came here. My parents had to contact the Witch's Council to get me back, and I will explain that in a bit. Once I put this on, it masked my powers from being detected. My father has special powers, as well as my mother. Yes, they are still alive. I'm sorry I've never told you that, but I thought it best that you not know the details. Again, not my best plan."

Now, Morgan had even more questions. Staying calm, she listened, hoping answers would be forthcoming. She tried to avoid thinking about grandparents that she thought were long gone and the loving family gatherings they could have had.

"There is so much to tell you in such a short time. I hope you don't hate me for keeping you in the dark about all of this. You won't understand everything right away, but I will be here for a week so we can get you all the knowledge you need from me."

She rose and wrapped her arms around her mother, who stood and hugged her back. Why hadn't she ever realized how thin her mother truly was. No words were needed as she felt the love she had never felt before from her own mother. Words echoed in her brain that all would be alright once she understood and learned.

Morgan held her mother at arm's length, warm tears trailing down her cheeks. "I have never hated you, mother. There were times that I didn't understand why we had a distance between us, but I never hated you. We'll get through this week. I promise I will listen." She reached for tissues for both of them and sat back down.

Annette calmed herself and sat quietly for a few moments. "I'm so afraid he will find you. I worried all the way here that something would happen before I could get the necklace to you. As long as you wear the crystal, he won't be able to know your powers have awakened now."

"Who is this person? How will I know?"

Her mother hesitated and wrung her hands. "He isn't a person. He is a demon who is hundreds of years old. I fear he's already here. Somehow, you moved to this special community of other witches. I hope one day you will find them so they can continue to help you learn after I leave."

Morgan smiled. "I have already found them, mom. I think they are anxious to meet you. They knew you were coming."

For the first time, her mother smiled back. "I would love to meet them...in a few days. I need to explain so much before then." She went back over to the box and pulled out an ancient leather-bound book with pages that appeared to be hundreds of years old. She handed the book to Morgan.

As soon as she touched the metal embossing on the front and the side lock, her fingers tingled and hit nerves going up her arms. Her mother still held onto the book. "That is how powerful the magick is that is inside the covers. You are now the owner of our family grimoire that holds years of spells and secrets. Your ancestors have written their knowledge here and now it belongs to you. One day, it will belong to Logan."

She sat further back in the recliner and slid her hands over the front cover as her mother sat back on the bed. This is the book

Suzy had spoken of that her family owned. The immense knowledge contained within these pages overwhelmed Morgan.

How will I learn it all?

"You don't have to learn it all. That's why you have the book now. Yes, I can hear your questions...and you can hear mine if you open yourself to that. There is so much, hon. Now, explain to me what happened at the store the other night."

Morgan blinked that her mother knew about the break-in. She stared at the ceiling, then at her mom. It was an ordeal to go through it all again, but she told her every detail and how Nate had come there to help her.

"Mom, all I needed to do was think about how it looked before it was broken, and the pieces floated back into place as if it were a new window."

Annette nodded with compassion in her eyes. "That's how it is. So be very careful of what you wish for...good or bad. That is why I didn't want you to have this ability, but you do. I couldn't stop it any more than you can stop Logan from having abilities. His powers have not been bound and if he hasn't said anything, I'm not sure if he has them. The two of you will have to talk so he is aware of what might be possible. That timing is up to you."

Morgan stared at her mother as thoughts of a confused Logan ran through her mind. "Mom, how did all this come about and how did you never mention any of this before now? I had to find out on my own. I don't get it."

"You are now in my position. Do you tell Logan or wait for him to ask you? Should he have powers and use them, the *demon* will locate him, and you'll lose your son. His powers need to be masked also." Annette stepped back over to the box and pulled out another velvet jewelry box. "This was made for Logan. The ring will size to his fingers as soon as he puts it on, and his powers will be hidden from those who want our family. I didn't think he'd want a necklace." She handed it to her daughter.

When she opened the box, Morgan saw a beautiful woven ring of silver and gold, with a basket-weave pattern. She moved her fingertip over the ring. "Who are these people who want our family and why? That's what I don't understand."

"Centuries ago, one of our ancestors, Margaret Scott, was burned at the stake, as they did with witches in 1692. Her family fought back and ended up making a deal with Dantalion's father back then so that no more of them would be prosecuted for witchcraft and they'd be protected. His father was a warlock who went to the dark side, as close to being a demon as a warlock can get, in order to control more good witches. Someone along the line no longer wanted to be under his spell and hid their powers to escape. As you know, dark warlocks never die, they just accumulate more souls, giving them more power. If they die, it's usually at the hands of another warlock or witch who was protecting their own life. Our family has been protecting the children ever since."

Annette rose and walked to the window where the curtain was pulled closed. She peered through a crack to see outside.

"There's more to it than this isn't there? Tell me!"

Without turning away from the window to face Morgan, her mother continued. "When you married Ken, he was mortal. That meant there was a fifty-fifty chance that Logan would have your powers, maybe not as powerful...maybe more so. Your father and I are both witches. Should Logan marry a mortal, the same holds true for his children. *You* will decide when the two of you will discuss this. Does that make it any easier of a decision?"

Morgan dropped her shoulders and leaned back in the chair. "No, it doesn't, but I don't want him to be in the dark about any of this. You said he could be more powerful than I am. How so?"

When her mother turned around, her brows knitted together, and her lips were tight. "Your father has many powers and was on the Council years ago. He left when they chose to release a few bad dark witches before they served their time, although he was totally against their release. Dantalion was one of them. He swore to his father that he would uphold the old spell and not let any witches escape the spell if he could help it. His father has since passed on, to hell, I'm sure."

Her mother sat back on the bed and watched Morgan closely. "Our decision to withhold knowledge of your powers was not an easy one. When you decide to tell Logan, it will not be easy to explain this to him. Especially if he's not experienced any magick yet."

Morgan closed the ring box and slipped it in her purse. "I don't want him to marry and not know what the possibilities are for his future. I'm glad I have friends and our coven. The women are willing to help me learn." She pounded her fist on the arm of the chair. "I just feel like a child where my abilities come in, since I have no idea what I'm even capable of! There is so much I don't know."

"As you read through the grimoire, you will learn more. Perhaps you and Logan can read through it together and explain things to him that way, now that you have the book." Annette wrung her fingers together then flattened her hands on her thighs, rubbing her fingers as if to warm them. "I drove here to meet you, but...in fact, I could have just teleported here via ripples in the atmosphere, but that might have set off other silent messages to the dark warlock. He isn't far from here. I can sense it." She touched her own necklace to be sure it was still in place.

"Teleporting? I've heard of that, but never dreamed it was real!" Morgan widened her eyes at the thought of having other powers she wasn't yet aware of. Suzy even suspected she had more abilities. *How does one sense that?* She pressed on her temples, wanting some of the inquiries to go away. "So, in the future, you will just teleport here and not drive? This is crazy!"

"I will always be a thought away should you ever need me. You and Logan just need to touch the necklace or ring to be in touch with us. That's the best explanation I can give you. Other than what's in the book. The demons and what they want is all in there. I hope you learn what you search for since I don't have all the answers."

"This demon...he has a name? Is he in town? Does he follow you?"

"His name is *Dantalion*, and he's here because your powers were like a beacon to him. That is why you must always wear the crystal. For Logan as well. Should magick come to him before he has the ring on, he will become a beacon also. Dantalion will have the ability to snatch him from you should that happen. Your father and I felt the dark warlock, that demon, last week, and knew it was time to tell you and get the necklace created."

Morgan shook her head and stared at her mother. "This is too much. My coven will be interested to hear all of this and perhaps they'll have some ideas of how to help me protect us better." Morgan sat forward with the book on her lap. "I want to get home and read some of this. Wait...can I also teleport? How is that even done?"

Annette glanced at the ceiling, then back to her daughter. "Giving too much information before you know everything is dangerous, so please be careful. You must envision the location you want to be at and know something familiar about it, like the room, or exterior, for instance. Then just think of yourself there. You will feel the magick through every nerve in your body before you go and then you're there. It takes practice but I'm sure you will figure it out. Don't ever teleport in front of a mortal! Go to a dark corner or outside in an alley. You and

Logan will have a connection once he puts the ring on. You can communicate that way as well, such as wanting him to call you or that you need to know he's okay."

She clutched the ancient book in her arms. "I'm really glad you're here, mom. Logan will want to see you. We don't need to talk about abilities but stop in for a coffee. He'd love to make up something special for you. I'll head home and let you rest. We'll see you tomorrow?"

The smile lit up her mother's face. "Yes. That's a great idea. Then I can see Logan and your shop. Please call me tonight if you have any other questions."

"I will." Morgan closed her eyes, thought about her own living room, and her arms and core immediately began to tingle. Her feet grounded where she stood. Then the air around her moved, and when she opened her eyes, she stood in her dimly lit living room.

Thoughts of the demon haunted Morgan as she stood in her apartment and touched her necklace. *I'm home and safe, mom.*

Teleporting could come in handy once she perfected that skill. She looked around, once again, glad she always left a lamp lit on a timer. Come to think of it, she'd always had a timer for her lamp.

She set the grimoire on her small kitchen table, along with her phone, and hung up her sweater. Then she felt the air change and looked toward Izzy's chair, as she'd come to call it. The old woman sipped her tea and nodded when Morgan saw her. "You have discussed your past with your mother. A good beginning."

Tea sounded good but so did a glass of Riesling. Decision made. Wine it is. Morgan poured her wine and went to sit with Izzy. "Where do I even begin? How much do you know that I don't need to explain to you? And who is this demon that's lurking around here?"

The old woman choked on her tea and nearly dropped her porcelain cup and saucer. The cup clattered as it settled. "Who told you that? Your mother knows about *Dantalion*?"

Chapter 10

Kinsley was glad she decided to spend the night at Rafe's after her encounter with the demon in the basement at work the other day. It had been a few years since their community fought together against the ocean demons who wanted more souls to take into the deep with them. So, Rafe wasn't a stranger to that world since he and his packmates had fought side by side with her.

A glass of amber liquid over ice dangled in front of her, and she glanced up at Rafe as she took it. "You were a million miles away. Everything okay?" He sat next to her on his leather sofa and pulled her closer. Just being near him made her feel protected and safe. Rafe would kill for her. She knew that. He gave and never asked for anything in return.

Yet her heart wouldn't take down the wall.

She savored the whiskey as it lingered on her tongue, then pressed her lips together and looked at Rafe. "No, everything isn't ok. Our internet went out at the office yesterday, and I had to go downstairs to check out the wiring." She swirled the ice in her glass. "A shadow figure was down there in the corner. His face was shrouded but his voice sent shivers down my spine. He said there is a witch in town, and he wants her. I had no idea who he meant, but now I'm thinking it is Morgan or her mother. I don't know what to do."

His jaw tightened, making the muscle tense beneath the skin. "I don't like any of this. I don't want you going down there anymore. Please call me so I can go down. I'll deal with him."

Kinsley did like being taken care of, and Rafe certainly did that for her. She ran her fingers over his muscled thigh, feeling the heat through his jeans. Tonight was theirs, and she didn't want to waste it on problems they couldn't fix right now. His windows looked out on the pool and hot tub on his deck with the woods beyond that. The yard was beautiful, and they'd had some good times in the hot tub.

She drank the last of her drink, and as soon as she set her glass on her thigh, Rafe put his fingers beneath her chin, pulled her face toward his, and his lips took hers. Whiskey melded together as his tongue moved over hers, sending heat to her core.

Kinsley kissed him back, not realizing how bad she wanted and needed to be loved tonight. Her fingers trailed over his neck and pulled him closer if that were possible. A moan slipped from her throat as her nails dug into his flesh.

When Rafe pulled away, his forehead touched hers and they sat for a moment, enjoying what had passed between them. She knew his need met hers, if not surpassed it. "You know I can have us in your bed quicker than you will get us there."

"If that's an offer? You know I won't refuse. I'm here to please your every need, woman." A groan slipped from his throat as he closed his eyes.

"Hold on tight." In an instant, they stood in his dark bedroom, the scent of leather emanating from his jacket that hung in the corner.

Rafe took her glass and set it on the coasters on the nightstand with his. When he turned back to her, Kinsley's fingers began undoing the button of his jeans, the skin of his taut stomach warm against the back of her fingers. Slowly, the zipper inched its way down, and her hands moved back to grip his ass in her fingers and pull his hips against hers.

His hands cupped her face, and he kissed her hotter than ever before as she slowly stepped backward. When the back of her legs hit against the mattress, she leaned them both back onto the bedspread.

Rafe pulled from the kiss, took her hands, and held them over her head as he straddled her hips. She gazed into his hungry blue eyes, his pupils larger than normal, then closed her eyes and pressed her head back against the bed. Her body betrayed her as she lifted her hips against him. The way Rafe melted her insides made her thoughts crazy. She had to admit how bad she wanted this man. "I can't touch you if you restrain my wrists."

Without a word, he held them in one hand as his other slowly moved down her side to her hip, as his thumb slipped inside the waist of her jeans. Soon, the top button and zipper were undone, and he teased deeper. The heat of his touch was like a hot iron, and moved over her jeans between her thighs, then slowly up her stomach, beneath her tee shirt and cupped a breast. His touch seared her skin as her need grew out of control.

"Your body molds right into my hand, woman. God, I want you." His breath warmed her neck, and his mouth roughly took hers. Kinsley struggled to get her hands free, to no avail, as she pressed up along his hardness. Their bodies soon stretched together, and his hand cupped her ass as his hips pressed hers into the mattress.

His need bulged against her. "You have no idea what you do to me when we're this close. You're beautiful."

Again, she tried to free her hands, but he held her tight. The hunger in his eyes bored into hers, telling her exactly how badly he wanted her.

"I'm going to let go of your wrists, on one condition."

She smiled. "And what would that be, sir?"

"You keep them over your head until I tell you to move. Tonight, you're mine to do with as I please. And I plan to please *you* first."

Her breath came in short gasps as she thought about all he could make her feel. "But..." She wiggled beneath him, knowing how heated he was.

"No. No buts. I get to spank your bare ass if you move to touch me. Understood?"

She rolled her eyes. "Fine."

Finger by finger, he let go, and his hands teased their way down her body, pulling her jeans down her thighs and off her feet, leaving a thong meant for his eyes only. Rafe tossed her jeans aside. He moved around to the other side of the bed and above her head. Her tee shirt got pulled up over her head and tossed while she kept her hands where he'd put them. Kinsley had never been so happy that she wore her matching lace bra and panties.

A groan escaped his throat as he made her wait.

As she looked up at him, Rafe peeled off his shirt, baring his chiseled chest and abs, then slid his jeans down. She loved that he went commando.

Goddess, he was beautiful.

The ridges of his six-pack met with the hairline that drew her attention further down, and she scooted closer to him.

When she reached out to cup him, he slapped her hands and gave a deep chuckle. "Now your ass is mine, baby! Roll over!"

Grudgingly, she obeyed.

After kicking off his jeans, Rafe slowly crawled over her body and slapped each bare cheek. Each slap stung, but the next two stung more. She bit her lower lip, and two more slaps landed.

When he raised enough for her to move, she rolled over beneath him and wrapped her fingers behind each of his thighs. Her lips pressed against his hardness.

"Woman!"

Her tongue touched him, and he gasped.

"Don't move...anything! Give me a minute." His groan satisfied her.

She reached higher to cup his ass cheeks and trailed her nails down over his muscles. The speed with which he moved shocked her as he sat up on the edge of the bed. He lifted her over his thighs. His arms held her back and legs, making her immobile over his knees.

"Rafe!"

"I warned you, did I not?" He lifted one of his legs to cover hers, giving him a free hand as his leg pinned hers.

The first slap landed, and she stayed quiet.

"You will count each one of these, up to five."

Kinsley gasped, surprised that he would go through with this. She played along. "One."

He waited, throwing her off.

What the hell?

Another slap landed, sharper than the first. "Two!"

She kept it up through all five. To her amazement, she was wetter than before they came to his room. Never would she have dreamt that being immobile and spanked could excite her to this extent.

His fingers slipped inside the band of her thong and peeled it down, his hand smoothing out the burn on her skin. When his fingers slipped between her flesh, he pushed, and her insides tightened.

Goddess, she thought she was in heaven as she arched her back. Without moving his hand, Rafe lifted her onto the bed.

"You enjoyed it, so don't bother denying it, woman. I have more in store for you than just that!"

* * * * *

Monday morning, Morgan dressed in black slacks and sweater with her dark hair pulled back. She arrived downstairs at the store early as the smell of coffee wafted through the air.

Logan had already opened the store for her and chatted with an older couple at their table. He glanced up when she walked in. "Morning, mom. Can I make you your special brew?"

"I'd love that, Logan, thank you." Morgan greeted the couple who were regulars. She noted that Logan had also made sure the fireplace had been turned on.

Her son had grown into a handsome young man when she wasn't looking. He'd inherited her blue eyes, and his dark hair fell over his brows. Without his help at the coffee shop, she would have had to put in so many more hours. Logan hummed as he made her drink and added a spray of whipped cream. "There you go, mom. Your raspberry mocha just the way you like it!"

"I'm glad that you enjoy working here to keep the customers happy, son. How are things going with you otherwise?" Morgan hoped he would tell her if something out of the ordinary had happened, but she doubted he'd bring it up here in front of the others.

"Mandy and I went to the movies this weekend. She's a lot of fun, mom. She had to be at work early today, too, so I didn't keep her out late last night."

Morgan knew that Mandy waited tables for her mom at the Krazy Locals Restaurant. Since her mom was part of their coven, Mandy likely had abilities also. She didn't dare say a word to Logan but knew the conversation couldn't be put off for too long. The last thing she wanted were for his abilities to be visible to this Dantalion guy.

She walked around the store to be sure the display tables were neat and orderly, enjoying her mocha as she checked the shelves as well. When she glanced at her door, thoughts of the break-in came crashing back, and she shook her head to rid herself of those images...and the magick she wasn't aware she possessed.

The bell on her front door jingled, and her mother stepped inside with a huge smile on her face. "I absolutely love this, Morgan! I had no idea it would be this cute, but you've always had a talent for designing the best."

She hugged her mom. The woman was beautiful and today she wore jeans and sweater with a black pair of flats. "I'm glad you came. Let's go back and chat with Logan. He came in early today."

Logan glanced up as Morgan and her mom approached. He hurried around the counter to hug his grandmother. "It's been way too long since we've seen you. This is a surprise." He looked at his mom and back to Annette.

She reached up to cup his face in her hands, turning his head each way. "You are such a handsome young man! Look at you. The spitting image of your mother."

"Can I make you up a coffee? Come have a seat. Do you want regular or something fancy?"

Morgan and her mother sat down at a small table so that Morgan faced the door to see as customers came in. Her mom's arrival had made her happy today. She wasn't really sure she'd stick to her word and come by.

"Logan, I'll just have a regular coffee with cream, dear. I don't need those fancy flavors or whipped cream in my coffee." Annette hung her purse on the chair and met Morgan's gaze as she curled her fingers over her daughter's fingers. "I'm so proud of you, Morgan. Logan has grown up so fast and now a college grad. Has he decided what he wants to do?"

"He wants to work with the local veterinarian since that is what his degree is in. He's waiting to find out when he can take his licensing exam now. Someday he wants to own his own business. I think they need another one in this area, but he's not said a lot about it. I don't want him to feel that he needs to stay close. He'd make more money in a bigger city."

Logan brought over Annette's coffee. "Wow! I do love the smell of good coffee! Thank you. Can you sit with us a bit?" Annette looked at Morgan.

"Of course, he can." The store was slow before noon and Morgan pushed out a chair for him.

"Logan, you've turned out to be quite the young man. College was good for you?" Annette sipped at her coffee while her gaze remained on Logan.

"I owe it all to my mom. She constantly told me that there wasn't anything I couldn't do if I put my mind to it. That's what got me through many of my classes. I always kept a vision in my head of being a vet with my own office. One day, I *will* accomplish that, but I know I have a lot of hands-on learning to do yet." Logan gave his mom a glance and smiled at her. "Thanks again, mom. You helped me get through."

Morgan's pride sparkled in her head. Logan had tried hard in college and made the dean's list several times. "I don't doubt that one day you will have that office so you can help pet owners take care of their fur babies."

They chatted about what and where Logan wanted to work. She watched their interaction, and it made her heart swell to see him with her mother. Neither of them had seen her for a while, and Morgan vowed to make sure they stayed in touch.

As the two talked, the bell jingled on the front door, drawing Morgan's attention to a possible customer. A tall, sexy, dark-haired man walked in dressed in a sharp beige suit. His shoulders more than pulled at the stitching of the material. His long curly hair covered his forehead and almost his eyes. The chill that rolled over Morgan's skin gave her goosebumps when she met his gaze. Her fingers touched the pendant with the tree of life, and his gaze followed her hand. She couldn't explain the look that crossed his face, but the sense she got about him didn't bode well with her heart.

The man walked around looking at the display tables, over to the bookshelf to pull out a book or two, then made his way over to the coffee counter. Logan hurried over to help him, and Morgan tried to ignore his presence to talk with her mother.

Her mother instantly changed, sensing something. "San Francisco could always use another veterinarian, you know. Then he could be close by for me."

"I want him to make his own choice of where he wants to live, mom. Although I'm sure he could make more money in a larger city."

The stranger approached their table. "Annette Scott? Is it really you?" The man's deep voice grated against Morgan's nature.

Her mother stared up at the man with such disgust in her eyes that the man should have been dead. Annette paused, as if she wasn't sure she knew the man. Her voice was just above a whisper. The man had attempted to take her hand in his own and place a kiss on the back, but she quickly pulled her hand from his. "What the hell are you doing here?"

"Now, my dear, is that any way to greet an old friend? And who might this beautiful young woman be? An acquaintance?"

"You don't need to know who this is. If you don't leave right this instant, I'll make your life a living hell!"

The man tipped his head back and let out a low laugh. "My dear, we both know that isn't possible."

The bell jingled again, and Morgan almost jumped from her chair. Nate scanned the store quickly, then saw her. He spied the gentleman and made his way over to Morgan, dressed in his uniform today. She'd never been so glad to see him and stood to greet him. "Nate, I'm glad you stopped in!"

He stared at the gentleman, who ignored Nate.

Nate smiled, but she knew it wasn't genuine. "I had to! I heard this is the best coffee shop in town." He walked over to the counter where Logan stood but kept his eyes on the stranger.

"Annette, I'm sure we'll meet again…soon. It's always nice to see you." With that, the man walked toward the front door, his deep laughter reverberating off the walls of the store.

Morgan could swear the air in her lungs got sucked out, and she gasped.

Her mom reached out to Morgan and fingers curled over her forearm. "Are you alright?"

She stared at her mother with eyes wide. "Who the hell was that man?"

Annette appeared calm, and Morgan was confused. "It's not important, dear. I really must go." She finished her coffee, slipped her purse strap over her shoulder, and stood up.

"I'll come back later, or you and Logan can meet me for dinner at that cafe. Let me know."

Before she could stop her, Annette was out the door and went in the opposite direction of her hotel. *What was she up to?* This wasn't like her mother. She laughed at herself. *Like I know what or how my mother acts these days!*

"Morgan, this is the best coffee! That was your mother, right?"

"Yes, it was." She looked from Nate to the door, and back to Nate.

"Darn it, I was hoping to meet her." Nate touched her shoulder. "You're white as a ghost. Are you okay?"

Again, she glanced from Nate to the door, back to Nate, and then looked at Logan. "I have no idea who he was, but he knew my mother. I've never heard her talk to anyone that way. I don't like this one bit."

Logan shook his bangs out of his blue eyes and curled his upper lip. "Mom, I didn't feel comfortable with him either, if that makes sense to you. Something is way too different with him. Something eerie hangs around him. I sensed it even before he came through the door." Logan gave a shutter.

Morgan shivered. "You picked up on that?" Her son may be more perceptive than she gave him credit for. "I hope I never see him again. He was just eerie. But I *am* worried about my mom, now. The way he looked at her was pure evil...just like his eyes."

Nate sipped his coffee. "Well, that helps to explain why I sensed something was off when I walked in the door. Do you have time to sit and talk for a bit?"

"Umm, sure." She sat down. Logan waited on another customer and seemed to have gone on about his duties. Morgan rubbed her hands over her forearms, as if the devil had just walked over her grave. She couldn't shake the feeling and worried about her mom. A dark vision formed in her head of her mother out at night and the stranger nearby. She shook her head, not wanting to alert Nate about the vision, but she'd have to discuss it with Suzy.

"There is no denying that Logan is your son. He has your eyes. I'm sure he'll catch the attention of all the young girls in town." Nate watched her intently.

She didn't know what to say. Her mind wondered where her mother was and what kind of trouble she might be in. Did her father know? Should she mention it to Nate? Concentrating went out the window. This wasn't like her.

"Morgan?" Nate scrunched his brows together and leaned closer.

She shook her head. "I'm sorry. I don't know what's come over me. That whole incident was weird. Thanks for coming in when you did." Putting her elbows on the table, she twisted her fingers, needing to think of something else.

"You know you can call me anytime you need to. Please don't hesitate. Especially now that I know this guy is roaming around and your husband is in town. Does Logan know?"

She sucked air into her lungs. "No, he doesn't. I'm not sure that would be a good thing. Then again, I don't want him mad because I withheld information from him. That's what my mother did to me, and I don't want him thinking the same thing." She glanced over at Logan, but he was busy making another coffee, appearing unbothered by what had happened. "He's growing up too fast for me, Nate, and he's not stupid. His senses are spot on. That worries me."

Nate knew she had abilities when she fixed the glass in her door the other night. "One day at a time. I'm sure he's smart enough to let his senses guide him should trouble arise. Was he close with his dad?"

"Oh, hell no. He saw the way I was treated by that asshole. Logan argued with him nearly as much as I did. He didn't think twice when I asked if he was leaving with me."

"Your ex's loss. He's a good kid." Nate finished his coffee. "I should go. I'll keep my eyes open for trouble and watch for that gentleman around town. Do you have plans for dinner?"

"With my mom, but I can call you once I get back home."

"That works. Take it easy on yourself. You've had a lot happen in the past few days." He tossed his cup in the trash.

Morgan walked him to the door. "I'll call you later. Thanks, Nate." She wished she had time to buzz by the gym to use their punching bag, but that would have to wait for another day.

Chapter 11

Rafe made coffee at the station Monday morning after seeing a slew of paperwork on his desk and the messages piled up. He didn't want to see who they were from, knowing full well it would not be the answers he wanted with regard to the cases piling up over the last several months. A killer terrorized his county, and there had been no word of sightings from anyone, nor clues left anywhere.

Soon, he'd have the governor on his ass if he didn't get the answers to the murders they've had to deal with. He didn't want anyone else to send an investigative team down on his neck to take over his own investigation.

With fresh coffee in hand, he headed toward his office. Nate walked in the door with a chip on his shoulder, but Rafe had his own problems to deal with.

"Looks like you need to get laid, buddy! What's the long face for?" Rafe had to get his jabs in wherever he could.

"I just left Morgan at the bookstore. Met her son. Nice kid. But there was a guy in there who seemed to be causing trouble for Morgan's mother. I sensed trouble before I even opened the door and once I got inside, there he was. Her mom and this guy had words, he left, and then she stormed out later. I have no idea who he was, but I've never felt that before."

"No idea who it was?"

"Nope. Morgan didn't know him either but said her mother must have by the way she talked to him. An old friend she didn't seem happy to see." Nate raked his fingers through his hair. "We don't need more people around here stirring up trouble. With her ex in town, possibly the one who broke into her store, now this guy causing problems with her mom...Morgan is a bit shook. She still hasn't told her son that his dad is lurking around."

"Keeping things from your kids never turns out well. She's well aware of that with her mom, if what we're hearing is true of her unknown abilities." Rafe went in and sat down, took a few drinks of coffee and spied the top message from the governor. "Son of a bitch!"

Nate stuck his head into the office. "Anything I need to know?"

"Just the governor with a request to call him back. We both know what he wants. We have no clues to the murders, nor do we know what's up with the missing organs from the dead bodies. I hate this!" He sifted through the other messages when he spied one from the coroner. "Maybe doc has info for me before I call the governor back."

"Good luck. Keep me posted. After coffee, I'm heading out to look for the ex in the gray pickup and maybe I'll see that stranger roaming downtown."

"You'll sense him before you see him. Just a heads up."

With a coffee in hand, Nate stood at his door. "Something I should know about this stranger?"

"You sensed him before you saw him. What you explained sounds like a powerful soul and not a good one. Watch your back. Stay in touch." Rafe picked up the phone to call the coroner, enjoying what he could of his coffee before bad news hit from the other end of the line.

"There is no evidence on this newest victim?" Rafe knew he was asking the coroner to withhold the death of Bobby Joe, but their community couldn't afford to have the coroner tissue-testing one of their own. Those blood sample would be off the charts with abnormalities.

"Clean as whistle. Just like the other two. I'd say the person you're looking for is OCD, has routines they follow daily. The cuts were precise, clean, and particular. This person might also have a medical background due to the findings of where the organs were cut. Very meticulous."

"Like a coroner?" Rafe laughed, but deep inside, he couldn't ignore the possibility. "A butcher, perhaps?" The owner of *Deadly Cuts* had already been on his mind, too. Then again, the fillet knives down at Bryce's building were also a concern, but were they too obvious?

"Rafe, if they are selling these organs, you have a bigger problem on your hands than just a killer!"

Muscles in his back and shoulders tensed as he hung up the phone. No evidence had been found at any of the scenes. Granted, the bodies had been found in the woods or on the beach, but no shoe prints were detected, no clothing left behind, no fibers found on any of the bodies, no family to contact.

"Sheriff, the governor is on line one."

"Shit! Thanks, Trish."

Rafe finished the last of his cold coffee. What he needed was more of that whiskey he left at home. Knowing he couldn't delay answering the call, he picked it up.

Twenty minutes later, he hung up the phone. He'd been able to soothe the governor, telling him he was calling in specialists to help with the investigation. He didn't mention the possibility of an organ harvester. A friend of his was already checking his connections for an investigator who specialized in forensics. Hopefully, they wouldn't have strangers crawling around all three towns. The war board on the wall showed body locations and names. When he sensed being watched, he turned toward his doorway and glared at Trish.

"Sheriff...hey, I might have good news, don't look at me like that. Someone just called to report that they found a cell phone. They said without touching it, they got it into a paper bag and are bringing it in. They should arrive in about fifteen minutes."

He couldn't help but get his hopes up. "Thanks, Trish. Get Nate on the phone and tell him to get his ass back here, now."

"Yes, sir."

Nate arrived well before the group of kids with the cell phone. "Trish said we may have evidence coming in?"

"Not sure yet where they found it. If it's wet, the info could be too damaged to pull. We won't know until they get here, and we question them. I doubt any of them are our suspects." Rafe raked his fingers through his hair. "The governor is anxious for us to come up with good evidence. He doesn't like what he's hearing on the news and in the papers. We'll have investigators combing the area if we aren't careful. I don't need the state coming in here, let alone the FBI. I have a call in to a friend in Portland. He said one of his guys knows a good investigator who might help us locate this asshole."

When the kids arrived, Rafe and Nate took the paper bag and led the hikers into a private room. Nate took notes on all the happenings of when they found the phone among seaweed on the rocks near the beach, their names and address. "Don't leave town for a few days. We may have more questions. You didn't see anyone else walking the beach?"

The oldest male spoke up. "There weren't any footprints in the sand and no one else walked the beach besides us. Tammy saw something sparkle by the rocks and then we found it. None of us have touched it."

Rafe had taken the phone from the bag with a rubber glove and placed it on paper towels. He stood up and went to the door. "We appreciate you bringing this in. We have no idea if this will have any information on it, but we'll check into it."

The kids met Rafe at the door. "With the murders happening, we thought it might be of interest. This stuff never happens here. Ever."

Rafe walked them out, thanked them for their help, and returned to Nate.

He'd finished taking notes and used his pencil to turn the phone over and move some seaweed. "The screen is cracked in several places. With it being in the water, I'm not sure we can get anything from this." Nate wanted to get this creep as badly as Rafe did. He also wanted to find Morgan's ex. That asshole needed to be taught a lesson.

Nate grabbed rubber gloves. "I'll pull the battery and sim card, then get this into silicone to dry."

"I'm going to call Mike in Portland and see if he's contacted that investigator yet. I think we need to get specialized eyes on this, and I don't mean the FBI. We'll get started on the phone tomorrow." Rafe walked out and back to his office.

* * * * *

Morgan, Logan, and her mother arrived at Krazy Locals Café for dinner. Katie's daughter, Mandy, had seated them at a table in a quiet corner of the restaurant. Logan and her mother got comfortable and checked the menu. Morgan didn't miss the exchange between Mandy and Logan and wondered if their relationship was a serious one. He sat so his back was against the wall in order to see the door and Mandy at the same time.

Mandy had blonde hair and blue eyes like her mother, and Morgan was sure she had also inherited her mother's magickal abilities.

Although Logan had never said anything about strange things happening when he was around her, perhaps she just didn't trust Logan enough to use them in his presence. Morgan had to trust that Logan would be careful and use his head. She didn't want any grandchildren just yet. Too many issues were still up in the air, and Logan still had no idea of what he was dealing with.

They gave their order to Mandy, and she brought their drinks as Logan got fidgety. He moved around in his chair in an attempt to get comfortable, but he kept watching the door and the windows.

Morgan curled her fingers over her son's forearm, and the tight muscles moved beneath her touch. "What is it? Do you not want to have dinner with your grandmother?"

He glanced from his mom to his grandmother and back. "That's not it at all. Something in my brain doesn't feel right. It's like the calm before a storm. Like something is about to happen. I've felt that for a few weeks now. What the hell?"

Morgan looked around. No one else sat near them. Dinner hour was still 45 minutes out. "Have you had this before? Like in college? Or just lately?"

Logan rubbed his palms on his jeans. "I never felt like this in college. I'd say maybe since we've moved here. Something in the air? I don't know. It's creepy. Like when that guy came in for coffee today. The same feeling has hung around since then."

Morgan looked at her mother, and her mother nodded, her blue eyes watching her with care. Morgan grabbed her purse and pulled out the ring box. She hadn't planned to do this in public, but with the man roaming in their city, Morgan couldn't take any chances, in case Logan's abilities were coming to the surface.

She set the blue velvet box in front of Logan. He watched her and her mother with suspicion. "What is that for?"

Annette leaned closer. "It's been in our family a long time, and since I'm here, I wanted to bring it for you. I hope you will always wear it. It would mean the world to me and give us a connection."

Logan slowly opened the box. Morgan peeked at it. The basket-weave gold and silver wound around a single amethyst. He glanced up at his grandmother. "Did this belong to grandpa?"

"No. Your great grandfather. It was my father's, and he wore it constantly. I hope you do the same."

Logan pulled it out of the box and slipped it on his right-hand ring-finger. "Wow, it even fits." He paused a moment and looked around. "It seems to have a calming effect. I like it. Thank you so much, Grandma. I'll always wear it."

Annette smiled. "Perhaps one day you can pass it on to your son."

Glad that her mother had come up with a good story for the ring, Morgan let out a happy sigh when their meal arrived. For now, at least if Logan's abilities were just now coming out, they would be protected. That didn't mean she could let their discussion pass for too long. He had a right to know.

Tapping his fork on his plate, Logan watched out the window. His attention went from the windows to the door. "He's coming into the restaurant. Too bad we can't hide!"

Annette's eyes went wide as she looked at Morgan. "He'll never know we are here." Her gaze went to Logan.

"Perhaps it would be good if he couldn't hear us, too!"

The gentleman walked in the front door of the restaurant, and Mandy greeted him. He looked directly at Morgan then around at the rest of those seated at other tables. "I'll be back later. I'm waiting for someone, but I don't see them here yet. Perhaps I had the wrong meeting time." The man turned and left the restaurant.

Now Morgan's eyes went wide as she stared at her mother. "What just happened?"

Logan leaned back in his chair. "Why didn't he see us when he looked right at us? I assume he was looking for you, Grandma."

"I'm not sure, dear. Let's finish and go back to your mom's place. I have another surprise for you, but it's at your moms."

Morgan shook her head, not wanting to do this tonight, but her mother insisted.

"I won't stay long. I promise." Annette ate her soup and salad as though no more discussion would be tolerated.

Logan shook out his napkin. "I'm fine with that, mom. Mandy doesn't get off work until eight tonight."

They remained quiet as they continued eating, and Morgan paid the bill when they finished. She hoped Logan would drive straight to her place and not ditch them. Tonight had not been her choice to tell Logan about his abilities, but it would be for the best. How does one tell their child they had powerful, magical abilities? He would surely think she had lost her senses.

Half an hour later, Morgan passed out wine and a beer for Logan, certain that he would need more than one. As her mother requested, Morgan placed the family grimoire on the coffee table, sat down and drank half her glass of wine immediately.

"That's a cool, old book. Is it yours, Grandma?"

Annette leaned forward and smoothed her palm over the cover, then pushed it toward Logan. "It now belongs to you and your mother. It's also been in our family for centuries. The pages hold many secrets that will answer any questions you might have."

"What questions?" Logan undid the small metal latch and opened the pages, slowly turning the parchment so it wouldn't tear. "This looks like a magick book witches use."

Annette smiled at him. "Why would you say that?"

"The drawings on each page are strange, like ancient drawings." He turned a few more pages. Dried lavender fell onto the table. He carefully put it back and turned a few more pages. "Holy shit, mom. This is a spell book!"

Morgan squinted at him as she cocked her head a bit. "And how would you know what a spell book looks like? I've never seen one myself until yesterday."

"Just from some of those paranormal shows I watch. A witch reads spells from something like this."

Annette set her glass on the coffee table. "And what would you do if you knew you had magickal abilities?"

Logan laughed at her, grabbed his beer, and sat back on the sofa to take a swig...then a second one. His gaze moved between his grandmother and his mom. Morgan froze, waiting for his reply. This wasn't exactly how she wanted to tell him this news, but it did get the conversation moving.

"That isn't possible because witches aren't real. You two aren't serious about this shit, are you?" He swallowed two more drinks.

"In the restaurant, when you said, 'too bad we couldn't hide', you cloaked the three of us so we were invisible to him. Did you feel anything when you said that?"

With a tilt of his head, he smiled. "Now that you mention it, I did feel something. Holy shit! It has to be harder than that!"

"Some spells are harder than that. I'm glad I was here for this. You are only twenty-one. Your mother is just now coming into her abilities, and I am to blame that she had no idea she has powers. That was wrong on my part and again, dear, I am so sorry that I kept you in the dark about this. I wasn't sure how to tell you, or if it would cause more issues, or if you would hate me for it either way."

Turning her attention back to Logan, she made direct eye contact with him. "There are others around us who go out of their way to make our lives difficult. They want our powers for their own benefit because it makes them stronger and will leave the witch or warlock with no powers at all. There will always be those who follow you. Please be diligent wherever you are, but as you know, you can already sense danger before you see it. That ring is not only a family heirloom, but it also hides your powers from the gentleman who came into your mother's store this morning, and others like him. He is a demon or rather, a dark warlock, and is hundreds of years old. His appearance changes to however he wants to portray himself. Do not be fooled by those who want to befriend you. Looks are not a dead giveaway, but you'll sense them before you see them, like at the café."

She waited for the information to sink into Logan's brain, and Morgan watched their interaction. Her mother had done an excellent job with her explanation, and she so wanted to hug Logan, but he appeared to be handling the news very well. Questions rolled in his brain; she could see that.

"Our family has had abilities for centuries. They are passed from parents to children. *When* they become active is what is not known. Your mother never showed any special talents as a child, so I knew by sixteen that she would come into them later in life. Your children will be the same. They may have abilities as babies or teens, or later, but you have the responsibilities to make sure they are aware that others want their powers. Your ring is more than a cover to hide your powers from the demons. Should you ever be in trouble, you need only to concentrate on your mother or me, and we will hear you. You will never be alone."

Logan twisted the ring on his finger, admiring the glitter of the stone and the gold. "So is the ring spelled?"

Annette smiled. "It was, by one who holds a high powerful place among our witches. There is a council, and so much for you to learn. This is only the beginning. Do not blurt any of this out to your friends. Some in this community are also witches...among other things. You should be able to sense those in the magick community, and it will become easier as you learn."

He looked at his mother with his brows drawn together. "Mandy is also special, isn't she?"

Morgan nodded. "She may not be aware of it yet. Her mother *is* a witch. When the time is right, the two of you will realize both of you are different. Many who live and visit here are mortal humans who have no idea we actually exist, and it must stay that way." She toyed with telling him about his father, but he had a right to know. "By the way, your father is in town."

Anger grew over Logan's features like a magickal mask, and his fingers whitened around the beer can.

Chapter 12

"Your father is a mortal, not a witch or warlock. He has no idea of our witch community or that my family has abilities. And he broke into my store the other night." Morgan explained it all to Logan, hoping he would understand that she kept it from him until she understood everything herself. "When I wished the glass to be repaired, it happened. I was shocked."

"And that is my fault. I hope my visit can heal all of us and a new understanding of what we are. We can't afford to be at odds with each other. The demons feed on that. Logan, if he knew at all that you had abilities, I didn't sense that. Your mother's powers are what he sensed...so far. When she unknowingly repaired her store, it was like a beacon to the demon."

"So, what do we do now? Is he going to be following me? Is Mandy safe? And her mother?" He tipped his head and stared with rounded eyes at Morgan.

"With the ring in place, he won't be able to track you at all. Please be careful." Annette finished her first glass and held it out for Morgan to refill.

Logan got up to grab another beer. "I'll be here for a while, mom. Another one won't bother me. This is all a lot to take in." Logan hugged Morgan as she stood at the counter then popped open the beer and drank before heading back to the sofa.

Morgan emptied the wine bottle and took their glasses back into the living room. "Mom, this is so much stuff. How can I train Logan if I don't know what I'm doing?"

"The grimoire has most of the information, spells to start with, and how to do them. I will be here for a few days. We can accomplish a lot of training in that time...in between you both working. The family history is there and how it all came to be."

After Logan left to pick up Mandy for the evening, and her mother went back to her motel room, Morgan texted Nate. He wanted to pick her up and go for a quiet drink to spend time with her. She liked Nate, and he didn't have a steady woman in his life. They could both begin a new relationship.

She wondered how he felt about her having abilities. He was there when she magickally fixed the glass in the door. Nate helped them train at the gym this morning, and he seemed fine with the others in her coven. She didn't know much about Nate other than all the guys seemed to be the guardians of their witch community. She liked that.

As he requested, Morgan waited inside her back door until he knocked, and she could see it was him through the peephole before unlocking the door. He stepped inside and leaned against the closed door. Before she knew it, his arms were around her in such a tender embrace and his mouth was on hers in a kiss that stopped her breath. Warmth is all she could think of right now and how right it was to be kissing Nate. She held his face in her hands and kissed him, their tongues teasing as they searched for more.

He slowly pulled back and put his forehead to hers. "I had to do that. I've been so worried about you when I can't see you to be sure you're safe." Nate put his finger beneath her chin to raise her face up. "We can head out now. I know you're okay."

"Thank you for caring." She looked up into his eyes in the dimly lit area by her back door, hoping one day their relationship might grow into more.

"You are so beautiful. I love that you're so independent and confident. That only adds to your beauty."

His lips were so close to hers. Begging for her to kiss them again. When she did, his fingers laced behind her neck, fisted in her hair, and pulled her in. A small moan escaped her throat, and his other arm tightened around her. She'd not been kissed like this in years. Morgan pulled away first, but not before touching his lips with hers a last time.

A few minutes passed as they stood quietly. Her insides funneled like a tornado with a need she couldn't describe, but she knew she didn't want Nate to leave. Morgan contemplated on just having drinks upstairs. Was it wise?

She offered her idea. "We could just stay up at my place instead of going out."

"I'd not suggest that, but since you did, we can if you're comfortable with being alone with me. I've already parked my truck."

Morgan reached up to relock the door as her heart hammered in her chest. She prayed she wasn't making a mistake.

Nate stepped out of her way while she locked the door. She was unsure of her decision, but she was glad she made it. Spending time alone so they could get to know each other was all she wanted right now.

Heaven had to create the kiss they'd just shared because it was that tender. She wanted more. One base at a time. Her insides hadn't been this excited in years. Nor had she met a man she wanted more than she wanted Nate. Time with him was precious with their work schedules, and she wouldn't waste it.

Morgan led the way back up to her apartment and soon he stood in her living room, kissing her again. Her lips as soft as silk, tasting of strawberries, and a body as warm as a she-wolf, but she wasn't a shifter, he wanted more. Nate pulled from the kiss. "I won't apologize. I can't help myself where you're concerned."

"I felt it, too. Does that make me a hussy?"

"You could never be a hussy. I love our chemistry even though we just met. Please don't ever back away from it." *Slow down, wolf! I'm not mating tonight. Get over it!*

"Beer? I don't think you drink wine."

"Beer it is." He watched her ass sway as she made her way into the kitchen in the open apartment. It was a cozy space big enough for her. "Dinner went well with your mother and Logan?"

"It did. I'm glad he got to spend some time with her. I hope she visits more often now that he and I are settled in here. She lives just outside San Francisco and owns her own jewelry store. It's been in the family for years."

Tonight would be relaxed, and he would let her know more about himself. He knew other shifters mated with witches so that shouldn't be an issue, unless she hated shifters!

Morgan brought them both a beer. She had a dark beer for him; hers was some fruity flavor and he teased her about it. Her laughter floated around them like a summer breeze. He would never tire of hearing it. Nate wondered about her ex and what he'd done to her that made her leave. He'd never ask her but would wait for her to explain. All in due time.

She turned on the television, more for noise than anything else, he assumed. They sat and talked of everything. "I've never married because I've never met the right woman, I guess. Never met a woman I wanted to know more about, until you. There's something that connects us, we just haven't discovered it yet."

"You're too handsome and built to be a single man on the loose. Another woman in town might already want you."

"Her loss. I haven't met her yet. So, you are the lucky one...actually, I'm the lucky one." Nate caught her gaze. "I feel comfortable with you. Not like I have to put on airs and be macho. I've nothing to prove, other than that I want to spend more time with you. I want to be sure you're safe with what's going on around us."

Her smile was genuine. "I feel the same way. But I hate that I don't understand my abilities. I need to read the book more to find out our 'family secrets' as mom called them!

Maybe I'm capable of zapping all assholes like the one in my store today."

The book interested him. "We could scan through the pages together if you care to share. Since I don't have a magick bone in my body, I certainly couldn't steal a spell from you!"

Morgan laughed again. "I hear that you are kind of magick though. I don't think I could shift into a wolf."

Nate paused a moment. "It's a good thing right now that you aren't a she-wolf shifter! We'd already be mating!"

Color rose from her neck to her cheeks like he'd never seen before. The color made her eyes even more blue and that's when he saw her thoughts rolling in her mind.

He couldn't resist as her gaze roamed over his body. "You're wishing you *were* a she-wolf, aren't you?"

Her hand covered her mouth as she leaned back and laughed until tears rolled down her cheeks. "Oh, my goddess, the image has me blushing. Stop it."

"I think it's a beautiful image...you spread out naked, just for me. Shit, I can't. I have to stop. You're right!" Nate sat back and got himself under control. His jeans seemed tighter, and he blamed that on Morgan. Hoping the beer would cool his demeanor, he took a few swigs. If he didn't contain the conversation, he didn't want to think what might happen, and tonight was too soon.

She also took a few drinks of beer before she stopped giggling. "I'm sorry. But thinking of you without *your* clothes is an even better image. Should we look through the book to keep our minds on other things?" Morgan set her beer aside and opened the book.

Nate's interest was genuine. He wanted to know what was actually in one of the books. He read the pages as she turned them. The family history went back centuries, beginning with those who had their children burned at the stake. He would never allow that to happen to Morgan. She was too precious to him. There were notes in the margins, names of some family members, a family tree, and something about hiding from the evil that surrounded them. It just wasn't clear what that evil was at this point.

Morgan scanned the information and kept reading as she sipped her beer. "This talks about the men in our family having stronger powers than the women, but it seems to skip a generation each time. That is crazy. To have the ability to blow your enemies away with the power of wind or water...or fire. I can't imagine how to harness something like that."

"It must explain it all if your mom wants you to read and find out. I knew you were special the day I met you." Nate used his finger to turn her face toward him for a kiss, which she whole-heartedly participated in. He set his can down and pulled her onto his lap as he leaned back with her. Tender kisses lead to deeper kisses. She touched something in his soul that he'd been missing for too many years.

He breathed in her strawberry scent. "You have no idea what you do to my insides. If we aren't careful, I'll shift right here and take you."

She leaned up and trailed a finger down the side of his neck. "Would that be so bad? We are both consenting adults."

Nate blinked. Had he heard her right? He couldn't do that yet...*could he*? Plus, she had no idea what a shifter was. He didn't want to scare the hell out of her, so that was out of the question tonight.

* * * *

A week later at the coven meeting, the women gathered at their spot around the fire pit in Kinsley's backyard. Somewhat hesitant, Morgan filled in the other witches of what her mother had shared, and she brought her family grimoire with her, hoping they could give her more insight. Although she hesitated to tell them about her son and his magick, she knew she had to. "Logan must be coming into his abilities because at dinner, he made the three of us invisible when the demon came looking for us. Just by saying 'too bad we can't hide from him'. Logan sensed him before he showed up. I'm thinking his powers might be a little stronger than my own. I never sensed anything like that at his age."

Kinsley already sat tense as Morgan told her story. "Dantalion actually made an appearance in human form?" Her eyes widened as she tipped her head to look at Morgan.

"He also visited my store and confronted my mother!"

"He knows your mom?" Kinsley shook her head and took in a deep breath.

"She said they had history and left it at that. So, I have no idea what that means since I know nothing of demons and their powers." Morgan twisted her fingers together, wondering what her suggestions might be. Her inexperience was beginning to be a hindrance, and she wanted knowledge immediately. Speed reading would be a huge help at this point.

Suzy spoke first. "We need to put up wards for your property. I know we also need to ward the rental cabins for Jenna."

"We need to get the spells together and find a powerful one since now we know what we're dealing with." Angela rose to stir their bonfire and push the coals to the center. "We need a banishment spell to ward off the demons from getting in. I have cayenne powder, lavender, and nettles in my stash to use with the spell. I'll also soak some basil in water to use at each location. These will work and need to be repeated every thirty days for a few months. I'll make enough so each of you have it that long."

Kinsley picked up Morgan's grimoire and went straight to the back where most spells were written. "When we do these, I don't want the townspeople staring down our neck, so we need to make this quiet. Let's do these after dark when most of them are in for the evening. Tomorrow night should work. Last night was a full moon and the waning moon will add banishment and stronger protection to the spells." She looked up at Morgan. "I'd be happy to help you go through these pages to learn so you can teach your son how to protect himself."

Relieved that she wouldn't be a burden on Kinsley, her mind filled with all kinds of questions. She wanted as much information as she could get, and she needed it now. "I've been reading it non-stop since my mother gave it to me. I had no idea our family tree was filled with witches and warlocks. I wasn't raised believing or not believing, but I'm not happy she kept me in the dark about all of this. I'd appreciate any, and all, help from each of you that you're willing to teach me."

"This demon guy is very powerful. Just thinking of him or mentioning his name can bring him within reach of your powers. I'm glad your mother had a necklace and ring blessed by the Aether for both of you. That will keep your powers hidden from him, and he can't track you. With that said, he now knows where you are and has made contact with you and Logan. When a demon is determined to grab the power of a witch, his mind is made up. He thrives on gaining more power, which elevates him in his society among other demons with each life he takes."

Morgan latched hard onto her panic. Logan must be kept safe at all costs. From what she read in the grimoire, he was destined to be an upcoming high warlock, and her father wanted to be kept in the loop on his training. "I need to teach Logan to keep himself safe. He promised never to remove the ring now that he understands what is at stake. He's been reading with me, but it's all a bit overwhelming for him...and for me. This is all too crazy and for my family to keep me in the dark...I just can't put *that* into words."

Jenna chimed in. "I've been doing the wards on my cabins and property for years. Any help in making them stronger will be welcomed. My family made sure I knew from a young age what I was and all that I'm capable of. Strong powers in our family are for glimmering and being invisible from others, so I will protect us that way as we put the wards up at both locations. Suzy, we can do your shop as well as Angela's."

"He came into my restaurant that day, too. I'm not comfortable with him roaming free. I want the wards on my property." Katie Parker looked at Morgan. Her blue eyes pooled with tears. "I worry about Mandy being with Logan. Please don't get me wrong. He's a great kid, but if he's being followed…"

Morgan's heart went out to her. "I understand. Logan and I have already discussed it. I'm not sure what type of powers he may have since he's not said a word to me. He had no knowledge of witches up to this point. Has Mandy said anything?" She hoped the blonde would be truthful.

"She hasn't said anything yet, so perhaps she isn't aware that he is a warlock. I'm not sure she knows how to sense the magic in others yet. Now I realize I should have been teaching her more than I have. I'll make sure she understands and work with her more. I promise. She needs to know that the atmosphere is off if evil is nearby." Katie nervously ran her fingers through her ponytail and smoothed over her hair.

"We all need to be on high alert. I'm not sure what is going on in our towns, but this isn't good. Be sure to work with each of your children so they understand magick is not allowed in the presence of mortals." Kinsley went back to looking at spells in Morgan's grimoire.

Angela rubbed Morgan's shoulder. "I'll get my herbs together so they're ready for tomorrow night." She had such a calming presence about her, and Morgan was glad they were friends.

Morgan's phone buzzed and she glanced at it. "It's Logan. Let me check what he needs. Hold on." She swiped the message open, and suddenly barbed wire wrapped around her heart. Her throat closed up as her lungs collapsed. After reading it, she dropped her phone and stared at Kinsley. Then she slid backward in her chair, and everything went black.

Suzy grabbed Morgan's phone, still open to Logan's message. She stared at Kinsley. "Oh, my goddess...I'll read this out loud...*I have your son, but YOU are my ultimate obsession. He'll not be harmed unless you ignore my request to meet me on the beach at midnight. Dantalion.*"

Kinsley reached out for the phone immediately, knowing she had to figure out how to deal with this demon. He'd made a threat toward Morgan last week, or at least that's who she thought he talked about the afternoon in the basement. There had to be a way to deal with this.

Angela was already splashing Morgan with ice water to get her awake and now keep her calm.

"I have to get to Logan, now!" She struggled against Angela's hands that held her down.

Angela kept her seated.

"My mother needs to know that bastard has my son!"

Kinsley closed the book and put it on the side table. "Morgan, look at me. Now." She waited for the woman to come to her senses and look at her. "We need to stay calm. This is what he wants. For you to rush out to save Logan without knowing what might lie in wait for *your* safety. We can't be in a hurry without thinking this through. I won't play into his hands. He's dangerous and poses a risk to all of us if he takes you."

She gave Morgan a few minutes to pull herself together. "Take a breath. Calm your thoughts and clear your mind of the demon. Do not think of him. He said he wouldn't hurt Logan. You have to be strong and sensible if we are to do this right. I won't let you just turn yourself over to this demon. Your mother knows him. We need to call her."

Morgan calmed down, and Angela stepped aside, letting her sit up. She rubbed her face and then her arms. Her hand then moved to her necklace and rubbed it between her fingers. She whispered loud enough for Kinsley to hear. "Mom, your friend has taken Logan and now he wants me."

Kinsley was glad she heard Morgan's comment. "You have a direct connection to her. She's a smart woman. We'll wait for her to get in touch with you. Here's your phone back, hon." Kinsley wished her mother could just teleport and join them out here by the fire.

Kinsley looked out over the water. The sun hadn't set yet and gave a red and orange hue to the sky. They had six hours to create a plan. A slight breeze blew past them, and the atmosphere rippled. An older woman suddenly appeared next to Kinsley's chair, and the woman reached out for her hand. Kinsley squeezed the gentle fingers as she looked up at her.

The woman's blue eyes pooled with tears. "I knew this would happen when I saw him in the coffee shop. My sins of the past are now catching up with me, but I had no idea my child would pay the price." She looked at Morgan. "I'm sorry, sweetheart. We will figure out how to get Logan back safely. Your father is working on a solution."

(Dear reader, you can go take a break, refill your drink, and come back. There is no Chapter 13, like there is no thirteenth floor at a hotel. Rejoin my characters in Chapter 14.)

Chapter 14

Tonight, Nate and Rafe were working late on the investigations when he suddenly thought of Morgan and whether she was safe. Something kept nagging at him as he re-bagged the phone and placed it back in the silica gel. It wasn't quite dried out yet. He stopped at Rafe's office. "I don't have a good feeling. Something is off."

"About those hiker kids?"

"No, it's just a feeling that I need to call Morgan."

Rafe leaned back in his chair. "I think she's at Kinsley's tonight. They had a coven meeting, something about Morgan and her mother with new information on her abilities." He grabbed his phone. "Let me text her."

"Thanks. I'll get this phone put away so we can work on it later."

The nagging worry got his wolf wound up. This didn't happen often, and Nate couldn't shake it. Sliding the box with the phone, battery and sim card onto the shelf, Nate stopped at Rafe's door. He didn't like the scrunched eyebrows and the way Rafe's lip inched up on the side. Even the veins in his neck stood out, telling Nate the news wasn't good from Kinsley.

"What's up? I can tell it's not good."

"The demon is causing trouble!" Rafe's shirt tightened across his chest, and he unfisted his hands.

"So, my intuition is spot on. What is it? Is it Morgan?" His insides clawed at him.

"Kinsley wants us to patrol the beach about ten and be ready for action at midnight. This guy has Logan, but he wants Morgan. He's obsessed with her. That's all Kinsley said. I have no idea what they've got planned. She said Morgan's mom teleported and is with them."

"Call Diablo. Tell him to bring Stephanie. We can use more shifters."

"We can stay out of sight and still watch out for this guy to show. Kinsley said they have Morgan's dad working with more powerful witches to help with this asshole. Not sure how they destroy a demon, but that needs to happen. I'm calling Diablo and then Mike." Rafe grabbed the phone and dialed.

"I'll be back in an hour. Keep me posted." Nate had to get to Morgan. He hated to barge in on their coven meeting, but he needed her to know he was there for her. After sending her a text, he jumped in his truck. The distance seemed to take forever to reach her. They'd just gotten together, and he refused to let this demon win. Morgan was his, and he wasn't about to share her.

* * * * *

Kinsley knew she had to keep her head on straight. Dealing with a demon as strong as this one would take more power than she had. "Angela, I think we need to do a banishment spell on Morgan, so he doesn't get near her."

"I'll go up to the house and get the items."

Within minutes, Angela returned with the small wooden dowel, string, paper, and a black pen. "When she has it done, toss it into the fire. Before we start, I'm going to reclose our circle of light, then we can begin." She had the candles blown out, and one by one, Angela relit them as she recited their prayer. After sprinkling salt on their circle, she turned to Kinsley to begin.

"Goddess, protect us this night as we protect one of our own. We will banish the demon tormenting her and her son. As I speak it, so it will be done." Kinsley took the items from Angela and gave pen and paper to Morgan, then glanced at her mother. "Please stand behind your daughter for protection."

Once Annette stood in place, Kinsley instructed Morgan. "Write down that Dantalion is to be banished from your lives, and he's never allowed to contact you. Then wrap that paper around this wooden dowel and secure it by wrapping the string around the paper."

She wrote the instructions for the demon, took a deep breath, and received the dowel from Kinsley.

"As you wrap the paper and secure the string, repeat these words three times. When you finish, toss the dowel into the fire.

> *Your bad behavior is going to cease,*
> *Thoughts of me, you will release.*
> *My feelings for you are as stone,*
> *I command you to leave me alone.*

"Think about the words as you repeat them three times."

Morgan did as she was instructed. Kinsley and her fellow coven held their arms toward the stars even though it wasn't dark yet. She prayed to the goddess for protection at the same time Morgan spoke and wrapped her instructions on the dowel.

Once completed, Morgan stood and walk toward their fire pit. She tossed the stick into the flames and with an explosion of fire, it burned blue high above the fire pit. She watched it burn, then turned to hug her mother.

A movement outside their circle caught Kinsley's attention. Nate stood patiently outside their circle. It wasn't the first time he'd witnessed a ceremony, and he waited to be acknowledged. "Nate, please join us."

He hurried across their line of salt, waited for Morgan to turn from her mom, and she rushed into his arms. Kinsley knew they were seeing each other, but she had to admit that she didn't realize the two had grown so close. Nate held her tight in his huge strong arms, kissed her hair, then took her face in his hands and looked into her eyes. Kinsley's heart went out to both of them, and she hoped their ritual would help some in deterring the demon they would face at midnight.

"I heard about Logan. I just want you to know that I'm here for you and will do whatever is necessary to get him back safe."

Morgan's eyes pooled with tears as her lips trembled with thoughts of Logan. Kinsley didn't have children of her own but knew Morgan's heart was breaking. Nate kissed her tenderly in front of all of them, then held her tight again and allowed her tears to fall. He was a good man, and it made her happy to see them both together.

She pushed back from Nate, her eyes still tear-filled. "I know you care. Thank you for coming. Kinsley has helped with the ritual, and my father will be here before midnight."

"Rafe and I will be down there patrolling, too. You may not see us, but know we'll be there. Text me if you need anything. I'll leave you here in good hands." He kissed her again and disappeared.

Morgan touched her mouth and met Kinsley's gaze. "You are strong. I know you will do fine when the time comes tonight. We *will* get Logan back without turning you over to the demon. We *will* banish him. Let's finalize our plans to place wards on the shops tomorrow night. Angela, you said you have the herbs and items we'll need."

"I'll put the basil leaves in water tonight and gather the others."

Jenna stood up with them. "I'll be sure we are cloaked from view as we do this."

Annette stepped forward, taking her daughter's hand. "We will make sure he isn't able to come near you again." Her mom kissed her hand, making Kinsley miss her own mother.

She made a mental note to call her later when this was all over. "Let's clear and open the circle, then go inside and wait for Morgan's father. Angela blew out the candles and gathered them for use at midnight.

* * * * *

Rafe grabbed the phone as soon as Trish alerted him. "Mike, thanks for calling back. You have an investigator that is good at what he does?"

"I do. I'll have him contact you. He's on assignment right now. Hopefully, he'll be finished next week. His name is Kai McGarrett, special forces and now a forensics investigator. Busy guy, but he's the best."

"I'll look forward to talking with him. Can't wait to hear his input. We need to put an end to these murders. By the way, do you happen to know anything about organ harvesting and sales?"

"That's a new one. Can't say I do. Is this something I need to check into?"

"I don't have proof, just bodies missing internal organs. Thought you might have heard something."

"I can check with one of our labs here. See if they've seen anything strange coming in, like an abundance of organs."

"Thanks. I'll keep you in the loop." Rafe hung up with Mike, then scrolled through his text messages from Kinsley for Destiny's phone number. Seeing her name even made him take a breath.

Damnit! He had to call her. Just get it over with!

Rafe tapped her number and waited.

"Hey *creep*! I don't recognize your number, so you have thirty seconds to tell me what the *hell* you want!"

"It's Sheriff Conley. Damn!" He had to laugh at her audacity, but then again, he'd never called her, so she had a right to answer that way.

"Oh shit! Sorry Rafe! I'll put you in my contacts so I know next time."

"That would be nice." The sound of her voice made his head spin. *Why the hell was with that?* He wasn't some teenager calling his girlfriend!

"How are you, Rafe?"

"I'm calling on business. Can I ask you a few questions about your job?"

"Of course. How can I help?"

"I can't give specifics, but when tissue samples come in, you do the matching for organ donors, right? Do you get any information on who the donors or recipients are?"

"It's based on the recipient list, but in most cases, I do know who the recipients are as well as all of the surgeons. Sometimes we know the donor, but that is based on blood samples and other testing for a good match. What is happening, Rafe?"

"I can't say at this point. Can you say if you've been doing an above average of organ sampling?"

The silence on the other end told him what he needed to know. "I can't answer that, Rafe, sorry."

"That's fine. I'd love it if you could come back to Pebble Cove soon and we can discuss all of this. It's quite important."

"Let me check my schedule for the next month and I'll get back with you. Does that work?"

"It does. I'll keep Kinsley posted. She'd love to see you again. Call me when you know your schedule. Thanks, Destiny!"

Done with the call, Rafe held onto his phone a moment, thinking what might happen should Destiny come back. He would need to be close to her again and he wasn't sure that would be a good idea. When his inner wolf clawed back at his decision, he knew it would cause a problem, but he had to get her answers to the organ harvesting.

Clearing his mind, he needed to call Kinsley. She wanted him and Nate to patrol, and Diablo would arrive about nine tonight. He'd never dealt with demons this close but knew that Kinsley had. In their wolf-forms and bear-forms, hopefully the demon wouldn't sense them, but Kinsley might have a spell for that.

His phone lit up with her picture. "Hey, babe. I was just getting ready to call you. How's Morgan holding up?"

"She's shaken up for sure. Nate stopped by a bit ago. Did you know those two are a thing? His feelings are strong if what I saw says anything. He said you two would patrol before we got down to the beach."

"We will. I hate this. A fight between good and evil. Not a match up I want to see, but we'll be ready. My wolf is ready for ripping something apart! Nate's is way overdue for revenge. Do I need to call in back up?" Memories of the battle with the California coven a while back didn't end well for the California side. Rafe remembered it well. They'd brought in demons hoping it would be a done and over deal. He still had scars from that, but he and Nate had helped push them out.

"We'll know more when Morgan's father arrives. I don't know him, but her mother says he has strong connections with the council."

Rafe could feel her stress through the line, and it tugged at his heart that he couldn't help more. "Diablo is bringing Stephanie. Her shifter side is nothing to mess with. They'll be here by nine. Stay in touch, hon. Let me know what's happening."

He hated hanging up with Kinsley. They needed a few days just for them, but now that would be on the back burner. Demons and organ harvesters were on his plate right now, and it needed to be over.

When he glanced up, Nate leaned against his door frame. Not much bothered his deputy, but tonight his eyes held anger and revenge. "I don't know Logan well enough to predict how he might be doing. I think he can hold his own but we're talking supernatural here. If he has abilities like Morgan, he has no idea how to use them or what he's even capable of doing. She's been working with him this week, but I'm not sure of their progress."

Rafe stood up and pulled out his keys. "Diablo is meeting us at my place by nine. Come on by, and we'll leave from there. We don't know where this guy is holding Logan."

"There wasn't a clue in the text that Morgan received. Just a time and where to meet. Watching her go through this is torture, and there isn't a damned thing I can do but sit by and wait." A nerve pulsed as Nate's jaw tightened. "I'll see you at nine."

* * * * *

"Morgan, do you know anything about using a scrying mirror? I have one. We could see if something comes through about where Logan is." Kinsley opened a desk drawer and pulled out an oval black mirror with a silver and black antique frame. She pulled a small stand from the back and sat it on the desk.

Annette stepped closer. "I know how...if you don't mind."

"Of course not. Please. If you have a past connection with this demon, it might work better."

Morgan stood beside her mother; a bit shocked at thinking one could see anything in a black mirror. "What are you doing? I've never heard of this."

"Again, I've let you down in so many ways. Let me do this and show you how at the same time. It's possible we can see Logan and maybe his surroundings to know where he is right now."

Morgan had thoughts scattering in her brain. Her only child was abducted by a madman and her mother now wanted to use magick. "If it will show us how to find Logan, good. What do I need to do?"

She sat down in a chair Kinsley brought over and looked at all the women who were watching how the mirror was used. Kinsley patted her shoulder to show her support.

Annette sat in front of the mirror and placed her hands on her thighs. "Close your eyes and imagine where your feet are, that you're sending roots to the center of the earth. Ground yourself where you are and feel the depth of the roots. When you're comfortable with that, imagine a calming white light around you and ask for peace and protection. Once you feel all of that, open your eyes and we'll begin."

She imagined the roots just as her mother explained. Her feet tingled and sparks moved along her muscles up to her fingers. Thoughts of Logan were put aside momentarily, and Morgan felt the peacefulness that energized her. When she opened her eyes, her mother was ready.

"I see a difference in your eyes. You feel it, too. You will be a stronger witch than I am, and you'll teach Logan properly. Your father will be proud when he arrives. Let's see what appears for us."

Morgan watched as light slowly swirled in the blackness of the mirror like a slow explosion. Kinsley and Suzy stayed close. Trees formed in a wooded area within the swirling light, then a bridge over a stream."

Kinsley gasped. "That's just outside of town. The water levels don't fluctuate much. Is Logan being held near there? Rafe and Nate can shift and patrol the area."

"Shift into what?" Morgan's brows knitted together in confusion. "I'm sorry, this is all new to me. Nate can shift into something?" Only a moment passed when she remembered. "That's right! We can use their help!"

"They both have the power to shift into wolves and patrol undetected by others. Some of their pack members shift into bear and cougar forms. I know it's a lot but hang in there with us." Kinsley squeezed her hand. "You and Nate will work well together. I need to text Rafe and give him this location so he can send Diablo and Stephanie there right away. They are also shifters. Maybe they can find Logan."

As Kinsley texted, Morgan watched the mirror. Suddenly, a horned goat-like creature came into view and the trees disappeared. The evil in his eyes made her gasp and straighten up in her chair.

Annette waved her hand over the mirror, the image disappeared, and she laid it face down on the desk.

Morgan blinked, unsure that what she saw was real. "Mom? What the hell? It looked right at you! What does all of this mean and who was that?"

Her mother faced her and took her hands. "That man who came into your bookstore the other day is not human. He is a demon who is hundreds of years old and can manifest whatever form he chooses. As he gathers others with powers and abilities, he then sucks those powers from them, and he becomes stronger. Logan doesn't have powers that we know of, but it's his way of getting to me, just as *you* are a way of getting to me. He's seen the glow of your abilities, and he wants them for himself."

"I've read about that in the grimoire, but this makes it real. I don't know what I'm capable of so how does he know what I can and can't do?" Morgan rose and walked out to the screened room to stare outside. None of this made sense and the anger built toward her family for not teaching her what she should have known all this time. Going back inside, she found her mom talking with Kinsley.

"Rafe will text back shortly. He said Diablo and Stephanie just showed up. They will go to the bridge outside of town, and Rafe and Nate will patrol the beach so they can be our guards."

Chapter 15

Morgan hated that her mother had put her in this unfamiliar situation. There was no time to read the book now. She needed to know what kind of magick she could do. "Why can't I just confront this Dantalion guy and get my son back?"

Annette looked directly into Morgan's eyes. "He is very powerful. There is likely a protective shield around the demon that none of us can penetrate, but if we catch him off guard, we might distract him enough to be captured. We're waiting on your father for that." She looked at the door to the screened porch when she felt the pull of a presence. "There's your father now."

Morgan wasn't sure if she was glad to see him or pissed that he was part of the reason that she was in this position and Logan was missing. He met her gaze as he walked toward them, and she couldn't help the anger that boiled inside of her. The space around her snapped as the electrical energy sparked. She fisted her hands in rage.

He carried a black briefcase which he sat next to where her mother stood. Her father rubbed her upper arms. "Morgan, I know you're angry. You have powers that you're unaware of, and they need to be controlled."

She jerked her shoulder, removing one of her arms from her father's grasp. "And whose fault is it that I'm not aware of all that I can do?"

Her father glanced over at his wife, then back to Morgan. "We're here now, and I hope when this is all over, that we can mend this issue between the four of us."

Her energy calmed some, and she allowed him closer, but later, there would be hell to pay if she didn't get the answers she wanted from both of them. Morgan vowed never to put Logan in this position. He would learn alongside of her, and they would conquer evil together.

After her father stepped away, Morgan had to bite her tongue. He knew best, yet she had to stand her ground on *not* being taught magick earlier. She closed her eyes to regain more control, took in a deep breath, and looked at Kinsley. "Kinsley, this is my father, Callan Scott. He used to be on the board for the Witch's Council."

"It's an honor to meet you, sir."

Callan shook Kinsley's hand, then turned to her mother. "The council gave me a weapon to use against the demon and disable his abilities for thirty days. They refused to give me the shackles to make him powerless so that I could put him into an iron flask and just be done with him."

Kinsley stepped closer. "Why wouldn't the council want him incapacitated for good. The iron flask would do that, from what I've read!"

"They contacted the Aether. He's the only one who can use the iron flask. I'm guessing this is a test to see how we deal with the demon, but I argued with them on that note. He needs to be shackled if nothing else and taken back to prison. I'd love nothing more than to be the one to do that!" He picked up the briefcase, set it on the table and lifted out the heavy wand. After pressing a button on the handle, the wand extended to three times its length. "This has a mace type spray that will make him fear us for thirty days and not come around. That will give us enough time to talk with the Aether so we can come to a reasoning and get this asshole back into prison where he belongs."

"And also give us time to ward the businesses and my chamber building before he comes back. Which, I'm guessing, will make him twice as mad as he already is, but at least he won't be able to get into my building any longer."

Callan looked at his watch. "We don't have much time. Do we know any more about where Logan is?" He looked from his wife to Morgan.

His blue eyes narrowed as he hoped for information and Morgan spoke up. "He is near a bridge and Rafe knows where that is."

Kinsley looked at her phone for additional messages. "Rafe is a shifter and leader of his pack. They are going to search the bridge areas. Later, Rafe and Nate will scout out the beach and be ready at the edge of the woods when we need them. He can easily sense the demon if he's in the vicinity. This is not the first time he's fought with me against the demons. I hope this wand can do the job, but we must be close enough to use it, right?"

Her phone buzzed.

"It's Rafe, hold on." She read through the message. "Diablo and Stephanie are leading the pack near the bridge and Rafe and Nate took ten others to the beach. They'll stay out of site, but one at a time will patrol the beach as lookout and be there when we arrive."

Angela touched Kinsley's shoulder. "The girls and I will gather what we need for the wardings while you guys go with Morgan. Come back safely."

"Thank you, Angela." Kinsley looked at Morgan and her parents. "We can all teleport to the beach." She held out both hands and they all linked in.

Her father held tight to the retracted wand. "Let's do this."

Morgan closed her eyes, too, as the tingling magick moved from her fingers to her neck and down to her feet. Once on the beach, she took a balancing step, not yet used to traveling that way. Darkness covered the beach like a blanket, lit only by the moonlight.

She sensed the wolves nearby as she wished Nate was with her. A comfort settled over her that he was there, yet the danger hung in the air like a heavy mist. She let go of her mother's hand and peered up and down the beach, wanting this night over with. It wasn't quite midnight yet. Her mind's eye started to fill with images of the demon near the rocks.

She wrapped her fingers around her father's upper arm and pointed out toward the ocean. "He's on the rocks out there in the water." Angry waves splashed water over the jagged rocks but never reached the top of the taller peaks.

The demon wore a white button-up shirt and dark pants as he sat with his arms on his knees. "I see you like to be early for your appointments, princess. I like that."

Morgan fisted her fingers as the air once again sparked with energy. "Where is my son?" she screamed out over the waves, but he calmly sat on the rock, shaking his head.

"Now, that would spoil everything, wouldn't it? He's safe from your shifters. They can't get to him." He stared at her as the energy drained from her face, then smiled. "You seem surprised that I knew of your friends."

Callan stood beside his daughter. "Be a man and come closer, or are you afraid of a witch or two? Perhaps you aren't even a man."

"Callan, my old friend. Your wife can tell you otherwise." His wicked laughter echoed across the short distance.

Her mother gasped and choked. "You're such a liar!"

"You know I'm not afraid of you, Callan. Just send her out here so we can consider the debt paid with her and her son. You stole the woman I had. I'm sure her daughter will taste just as sweet as her mother, and her son will give me the additional powers I need once I finish with him."

"The council won't let you get away for long."

"You know the council can't hold me and my powers. They've already tried that."

Morgan stood her ground. Determined to keep everyone safe, including her son, she knew what she had to do. It was for the best. *Nate will understand.* "Come over here to us, let my son go, and I'll go with you."

Her mother objected, but Morgan held out her hand to warn her mother. "This decision is mine alone to make. I'll go with him to keep this community safe!"

Callan also objected. "You'll do no such thing!" He shook the wand, pushed the button, and extended it to the full length. "Come ashore. You and me. Fight me like a man, you coward. Don't cower behind a veil and fade away."

The demon disappeared from the rocks.

Morgan's right arm was nearly jerked from the socket as another strong arm went around her neck, pulling her tight against muscled abs. "You are mine and the sooner you realize that, the better, princess." The hot whisper at her ear brought bile into her throat and the burn choked her more than the arm on her neck. She struggled against him, tugging at his arm against her throat. Dantalion stepped back toward the water, facing her parents.

From the edges of darkness, she saw wolves pacing behind them, their heads down as they salivated for the kill. Morgan's stomach knotted with fear for her friends. Then one huge wolf dove toward her as she was pulled back into the water. When the lone wolf attacked the demon, she was thrown aside. Dantalion grabbed the wolf by a front leg and swung it out over the water toward the rocks. The animal bounced off one protrusion, only to land on top of another jagged rock.

As the demon laughed, Morgan let out a scream that came from her toes, up through her entire body. All she could think of was Nate as she fought to stand up in the thigh deep water. The shifter had to be him that had been tossed against the jagged edges. She stared from the rocks back to the demon and narrowed her eyes. "You bastard!"

When Morgan pointed at Dantalion, electricity surrounded him and threw him backwards onto the sand. As he leaned up on his elbow, a second jolt of electricity knocked him back.

At the same time, her father took two steps toward Dantalion with the wand as the mist covered the demon. His deep screams echoed against the forest line and out over the water. "You bastard, Callan. Now *who* is the coward? You fight a one-sided duel. Now you're a liar, too!" He rubbed his eyes. "You've not heard the last from me. I'll be back, so watch over your loved ones."

Callan backed away from them as the wolves circled Dantalion. When he spun around, he suddenly disappeared, leaving the wolves howling into the night. Morgan dove deeper into the ocean and made her way toward the wolf on the rocks. A bare-chested Rafe beat her there, and she was too shocked to say a word.

When he touched the wolf, it shifted to human form right in front of Morgan. His arm hung at a weird angle from his bloody shoulder, and she clung to the rocks among the waves. Rafe took hold of Nate's good arm to lift him off the rocks and Nate's side seeped blood from the deep ragged cuts along his ribs.

Morgan braced herself among the rocks and raised up her arm. "Rafe, take my hand and hold on to Nate." When he reached out to her, she held tight, closed her eyes, and envisioned the sandy beach. The tingle rushed through her body, making her forget the cold swirling water, and soon all three of them lay on the dry sand.

Nate was unconscious, bleeding onto the sand and tears blurred her vision. Would he leave her before they even had a chance of becoming closer? Watching him die would tear out her heart. The poor guy lay naked and bleeding but had the chiseled body of warrior. When Morgan waved her hand, two blankets appeared from thin air. Her abilities still shook her that all she had to do was think of what she needed, and it could appear. Morgan covered Nate with one, and gave the other to a naked Rafe, who knelt at his friend's side.

Her parents quickly came over to them, and her mother's hand touched Nate's bad shoulder as her thin fingers moved carefully over his broken skin. She murmured words Morgan had never heard before, but knew it was a healing spell. Her mother looked her way. "Morgan, place both of your hands on my shoulder. Together, we are stronger."

Morgan put both of her hands on her mother as she requested. Her mother manipulated the bones back into place with her frail fingers, and Nate groaned, but didn't open his eyes. His wounds stopped bleeding, and with her own eyes, Morgan watched the torn flesh mend together and scar, then totally disappear. Fingers moved over his abs to the wounds on his ribs. In a few minutes, the wounds there healed the same way.

Morgan supported her mother when she fell sideways against her and passed out. Kinsley moved to kneel next to Morgan, then laid her hands over top of Morgan's. "She used *everything* to heal Nate. She will recover in a few minutes. Your mother is a strong woman. Not all witches can heal."

"Thank you." Morgan saw such compassion in Kinsley's eyes.

Kinsley searched around. "Callan! Hurry over here!"

Her father sat in the sand, then pulled his frail wife onto his lap. "Annette?" He gently caressed her cheek and brushed her hair back. Not often had she seen her parents show affection and it was beautiful. She'd never witnessed a witch heal someone. The process took all of their energy, and Morgan had never seen her mother so weak.

"I just got a message from Diablo!" Kinsley shouted to them. "They have Logan and he's fine. They'll take him to my place."

Morgan's lungs burned from holding her breath, and she breathed in deep as the news penetrated. Her friends were now like family, and they would have given their life, she was sure. She moved to comfort Nate, hoping he would recover. "Thank you, Kinsley. Rafe, please thank your pack."

"You can thank them yourself. They'll be there when we arrive at Kinsley's." He knelt next to Nate and gave him a gentle shake.

Morgan took Nate's hand and squeezed it as she called his name. His skin felt like ice, and she ran her fingers over his cheek. "Nate, it's over, but you're going to hurt some." He turned his head and groaned. Slowly, his eyes opened.

Morgan touched his chest to feel his heart. If he wouldn't open his eyes, she needed to feel that his heart still beat. Her fingers brushed away the sand and threaded through the hair on his chest to feel a strong beat. When she glanced back at his face, he blinked, trying to focus, then met her gaze and a slight smile curved his cut lip. "Welcome back."

He glanced at Rafe and back to Morgan. "Is it bad if I say I don't remember anything?"

"Not at all. It's for the best. No worries." Her fingers caressed his jaw. Her vision blurred from pooling tears, and the warmth trailed down her cheek.

Nate reached up and wiped her tears with the pad of his thumb. "It's going to be okay, even though I'm not sure what has happened, but I'm still here for you."

Her throat burned from unspoken words. How could she voice that he'd scared her to death thinking he might be dead? She leaned her cheek into the palm of his hand, thankful he was alive.

"Are you going to lay around like an invalid all night?" Rafe laughed as he tucked a corner of the blanket at his waist, then held out a hand to help Nate up. "Take it slow. We don't want you dizzy, or naked, so hold onto that blanket before you scare the women!"

Morgan quickly grabbed the blanket to help him get it around his waist. Nate wobbled a bit as he held onto Rafe and Morgan. Her father helped her mother stand, who was just as unstable as Nate appeared.

"I think we all need to regroup at my place and get some clothes for these two warriors."

Kinsley winked at Rafe as she went to stand at his side for support.

Callan grabbed Morgan's hand. "I'm going to take your mother home. She'll be as good as new in an hour or so."

"Thank you for what both of you have done for us, dad." She hugged her parents, knowing full well tonight was not a night for anger. "Nate may have bled to death if you hadn't saved him, mom. I can never repay that."

Annette kissed her daughter's cheek. "It's what mothers do, my dear." She touched Nate's arm. "Please take it easy for a few days. You were quite broken, son. You saved my daughter from the demon...for now. He *will* return, but we'll be ready when he does." Annette took her husband's hand so they could teleport together. Morgan would be forever grateful to her mother's healing abilities.

"I can only say thank you for bringing me back from death's door." Nate took in a deep, healing breath as he looked at Annette.

She reached up to hug the shifter. "Take care of my daughter, Nate."

Witnessing the tender moment between the man she loved and her mother, Morgan let the walls around her heart be lowered for a short time. Even though they'd basically caused this problem, the two truly helped out today.

"Morgan, hug Logan for us. I'm glad he's safe. Your mother and I will call later. I'll be in touch with the council about what we do from here."

She nodded to her father as she supported Nate at her side. "I'll call later. Thank you for your help." Her parents closed their eyes, and the atmosphere gave a static ripple as they left.

"Shall we do the same and get a strong drink into all of us? I'm sure we could use it!" Kinsley took Morgan's hand in hers, and she, in turn, held onto Nate.

Morgan still couldn't fathom what magick afforded her. The future would be interesting, but for now, she needed to hold Logan to be sure he was safe.

As soon as Kinsley stood in her own living room with her friends, she stepped over to her bar and set up four glasses.

"Don't even think you're leaving me out of this toast! I've been on pins and needles waiting to hear from someone about what has been happening and if Morgan and Logan were safe!" Angela stepped over to hug Morgan and set a glass for herself. "I wish I could have been there to help."

"You'll help when we ward my store and home...as well as Nate's home must now be included when we do this. That bastard has vowed to return, and now we only have thirty days before he has powers again to do anything."

Kinsley poured them all a good portion of whiskey. She handed out the glasses at the dining room table where the others had taken seats. "Before we toast..." she swirled her fingers and clothes for Rafe and Nate appeared in her arms. "As much as I hate to cover up such masculinity, you two can go change first so you're comfortable. We'll wait." She handed the shirts and pants to Rafe and watched his muscled shoulders move as he helped Nate toward the bathroom to change. The man was built like a god. Again, her mind wandered to where her heart sat, surrounded by the tall walls she'd kept up. Any woman would be glad to snatch him away if she didn't make a decision soon.

Why was she holding back?

Angela cleared her throat, and Kinsley snapped her head around to see her snickering. "I'm surprised your eyes are still in your head!"

Kinsley's cheeks and neck heated. "What can I say...other than they better hurry because I need that drink!"

Nate and Rafe left the bathroom just as a knock came at Kinsley's front door, and Rafe opened it. "Diablo!" Rafe hugged his broad-shouldered friend, then shook his hand. "Thank you for what you and the pack have done for us. Come in and join us for a stiff drink. Tonight, we all deserve it." He stepped back for them to enter.

When Logan came in, he searched for his mother at the dining room table. Kinsley's heart strings tugged as she watched the two hug each other. Logan stood a head above his mother and kissed the top of her hair. The two had quickly found a spot in her heart, and she would do whatever necessary to keep them safe as they traveled along the magick trail of abilities.

Rafe poured a drink for Diablo and Stephanie. "Had it not been for you two, Logan might not have been found. I'm glad Annette located the vicinity, but you two found him."

Logan's dark hair nearly covered his blue eyes, and he shook his head sideways to get the bangs out of the way. "I could use a beer, if there is one."

Kinsley gave him a big smile. "I happen to have a few." She grabbed one from the fridge and Logan popped it open. The young man amazed her as she wondered what type of abilities he would show them. It sounded like he may have a treacherous future if what Morgan learned from her grimoire was true. It spoke of Logan being a protector, and she hoped she would be around to witness that. His broad shoulders were filling out and his structure wasn't as big as Rafe or Nate...yet. One day soon, Morgan would have a lady-killer on her hands.

She loved having a home filled with friends and knew she was lucky. Kinsley reached for her glass. "To everyone's safety tonight! May we always return from our adventures!" The familiar burn of the whiskey, and the after-bite, is what she craved.

Everyone else had done the same. She noticed that Nate and Morgan held hands, and she smiled to herself, glad they might find happiness in the future.

Logan sat the empty can on the counter. "Mom, I'm heading home. It's been a bit of a crazy night. Diablo took me by my apartment to pick my truck up on the way here. I'll call you tomorrow. You good?"

Morgan moved to give him a hug before he left. "It's late, so be careful driving. The danger won't bother us for thirty days. We'll figure this out, son." She closed the door behind Logan and met Kinsley's gaze. "I think I'm with Logan. It's been a long night. Nate is better, and I'm exhausted."

Kinsley wrapped her arms around Morgan. "You'll be alright being alone tonight? You're welcome to stay here."

She shook her head. "I'm good. I'll teleport and be in bed as soon as I get there. This magick thing is kind of handy. Thank you for everything."

"Wait a minute before you leave." Nate slowly stood and took a minute to take a step but made his way to Morgan. "I'll walk you out."

"You both take care." Kinsley closed the door behind them and looked at Rafe. "I like the fact that those two are getting closer."

"He deserves a good woman, that's for sure." Rafe held out his arm and scooped Kinsley in to stand beside him. "I'm glad *I* found a good woman."

He kissed her cheek, and his warm lips sent her thoughts upstairs. His nearness melted her, and she berated herself for not giving all of herself to the man who gave all to her.

Nate came back inside alone. "She said she'd text you when she got home and settled. At least there isn't the possibility of more danger for her tonight."

Diablo and Stephanie had also left. It'd been good to see the two of them again. Kinsley made a mental note to ride over to Hagstone Cove for a drink with them. She'd not had her bike out for a ride and what better reason than to see them soon.

Angela had already gathered the glasses and set them by the dishwasher.

"Thank you, hon." Kinsley admired her auburn-haired friend. She'd been there through thick and thin, demon battles and witch training. Angela was indeed someone special and was happy that she had moved into Kinsley's home.

A smile reached Angela's blues eyes as she winked. "I'm glad everyone made it back safe, and that evil bastard is gone for a while. Perhaps the council can find him while his powers are depleted for thirty days and get him locked up."

"I hope Morgan's dad can get his hands on whatever spell can stop him." Kinsley pushed in the dining room chairs to the table.

"I have all the herbs and basil water that we'll need for tomorrow night. I can't wait to get the wards up."

"I'll see you tomorrow, babe. I'm going to run Nate home. He needs a good night's sleep to recover. Annette did an amazing job of healing him. I'm glad she was there."

Rafe had threaded his fingers into the hair at her nape and pulled her close. His warm lips weakened her knees. Disappointment fluttered through her mind, but Nate did need to be home. There would be other nights for them.

Angela gave Nate a hug before they left and soon, she and Angela made their way upstairs.

"I hope you sleep well after what you probably witnessed tonight. I'm glad Logan and Morgan made it through all of that."

"Me, too. Sleep well, Angela." Kinsley changed and then glanced out her window before closing the blinds. The sound of ocean waves crashing against the rocks beyond her backyard drifted on the night air. Bright light from the full moon shone down to kiss the ocean waves in the dark of night as the white caps floated over the water. Tonight had been more than a warning of what the future held for all of them. She prayed they could find a solution before lives were lost.

Kinsley pulled the string to close the blinds and climbed beneath the cool sheets. They were a welcome contrast to her overheated body as she thought of Rafe before closing her eyes.

Chapter 16

The next evening at midnight, with the waning moon above them, the women met at Suzy's antique shop and Kinsley prayed to the goddess to keep them safe. She watched over Jenna as she cloaked them with her invisibility spell so they could work undetected by the mortals walking around after dark. Once she'd done that, Angela accompanied Suzy outside to sprinkle salt and basil water around the perimeter and doorways.

Kinsley took in a breath and cast the protection spell over the store. She reached out with her senses to be sure nothing lingered. "We're good here. Let's head to Morgan's bookstore next. Then I want my building for the Chamber warded also. He's already been in the basement there."

Within hours, each of their businesses had been warded as well as Rafe's home and Jenna's cabins. Kinsley wouldn't worry anymore when she visited Rafe's place. "Now he won't be able to enter any of our establishments."

"Since I'm so new, how will he know that he can't enter?"

Kinsley's heart went out to Morgan as she felt her insecurities as the night mist from the ocean crept through town and cloaked them by the building. "He will feel it before he gets to the door of each one of our businesses. He has to expect this at some point. He knows we're all aware of his presence. I'm worried who else he may bring here to help him accomplish whatever it is he wants."

Morgan shifted her weight from one foot to the other where they stood on the sidewalk outside of the Krazy Locals. "I trust that we will all be safer now. I'll keep reading and studying what I need to, and Logan will, too. Thank you all for helping us."

Angela gathered up the bag of herbs left over. "We all need protection against any demon set on taking one of ours. I have more herbs and basil water when you run short."

Suzy touched Morgan's arm. "If you're ready, I'll go with you. I need to know you get home safely, and then I'll go from your place. Ready?"

"I'm still new at this, but it's worked before."

"Trust me. You can do this." She put her hand on Morgan's shoulder. "Close your eyes and envision yourself standing in your living room at home."

Morgan looked at Kinsley, and she nodded her approval. "Thank you again." She closed her eyes and thought of her living room. A slight electricity came up from her feet, through her core to her arms and seemed to tingle her fingers. When she opened her eyes, she stood at home with Suzy by her side. With wide eyes, she looked around then looked at her hands, then glanced at Suzy.

"I knew you could do it. You just need to trust in your abilities more. They will serve you well once you do more reading about what you're capable of. You're home safe. I'm teleporting home. Bye, hon."

Their air rippled around her, and Suzy was gone. Morgan immediately sensed Izzy and her gaze went to the chair. The old woman smiled up at her. "I have so many questions for you. Are you aware of what's been happening around here?"

Izzy laughed out loud. "My dear, there isn't much I miss. I especially like your shifter. He's powerful when he shifts. You need to trust him. He does love you."

Morgan gasped. "Please tell me you don't lurk in the corners when he's here!"

A smile was her only answer.

"I better not sense you around when he comes over next time."

"I don't need to lurk in the corners, my dear. My senses go deeper than that. I know what people feel and his feelings are strong for you. Trust him. Your souls will heal each other. His is pretty damaged."

With that, the old woman disappeared. Morgan searched the living room and kitchen. There were so many questions for Izzy, and she left her with a strange comment. *Nate has a damaged soul? Was his heart broken, too?* Izzy was nowhere to be found, and Morgan headed to her room for bed.

The remaining coven members laughed together. "I'm glad she's coming into her abilities. She will be fine. Let's all be safe tonight. Thank you for your help, Angela. Ready?" She and Angela teleported back home, as did the others.

Once in the kitchen, Kinsley shook off the sparks of teleporting. "I think we did a good thing tonight. I hate to think we need to watch over our shoulders for a demon as well as a killer now."

"I feel better now the wards are in place. The demon can't reach us for thirty days. I wonder what the extent of friendship is between him and Morgan's mother."

Kinsley chuckled. "I doubt it's a friendship. It sounded more like a curse to me. Morgan has so much to learn. Especially if she and Nate have a relationship. After what she witnessed last night at the beach, now she knows shifters are a real thing. What a way to come into your powers. I'm just glad her mother was there to heal Nate. She had no idea her mother was a healer. That's just not right on their part."

"No, it's not. She does know we're here for her, so I hope she won't hesitate when she needs help. I'm off to bed. I have inventory to unpack in the morning." Angela went upstairs.

Kinsley poured herself a whiskey to take up with her, first, adding ice to her glass. She'd been occupied all day and not talked with Rafe. He was busy with the investigations and trying to figure out what was happening.

* * * * *

Javier's number came up on my phone. Warily, I answered it. "Hello?"

The pause on the other end of the line was bone chilling. My stomach flipped as I tried to think.

"Are you not hiding the bodies well enough, asshole? This shit is all over the news! I'll kill you myself if you don't get caught first!"

The gravelly voice sent chills up one's spine. "I'm sorry, Javier. I'll do better. I didn't expect anyone to fish the body out of the water!"

"Don't *ever* use my name on this phone! Keep this shit up and *you'll* be dead. And I'll send them *your* internal organs! The next shipment is needed in three days. Don't fuck this up again! The boat will be waiting at midnight."

The phone disconnected, and with a shaky hand, I placed it on the nightstand.

Too careless!

You need the money, stop screwing up!

I paced off steps across the floor, from window to window of the old cabin. The clock glowed two am. A victim would be needed in three days' time. The chosen male had made himself available for grabbing and sat, tied up, in the back room. He was new in town and had stayed at the cabins down by the marina. No one would ever miss him.

Careful planning was needed not to get caught.

A noise caught my attention.

Banging came again from the back room. The man had been fed, but now made too much noise. His time couldn't come soon enough. The bodies had to be kept alive as long as possible, yet feeding a victim took too many chances.

No more grabbing victims before deadline! Feeding them took too many chances.

The truck was already gassed up for the trip to the other town where the boat would pick up the cooler. So far, all the drops had gone well, just the discovery of the bodies had to change. Better hiding places were needed.

The money was too good not do this, and it helped those in need of new organs. Thoughts of their mother and how long she'd suffered came to mind and then the anger took over. Pacing steps increased to wear a path between the windows.

It was never about the fear of getting caught. It was the fear of not helping others live a better life than they'd been dealt, just their mother had to, and no one cared. Bending in the corner, a rug was tossed aside, and two boards removed. Feeling further in, the box still rested where it had been hidden. *Relief.* Returning the boards and the rug, steps began again.

Pacing, back and forth.

No one had suspected they were being watched, so it had to be quick again, but not careless. Where would the body be placed this time? Deeper in the woods and off the beaten path. The captive would be gone soon.

Mother would be proud.

So many had been helped these last few months. With a deep cleansing breath, the bed sank down, and the covers warmed again.

Three more days.

* * * * *

Rafe slammed down his coffee cup, hating that his own men couldn't solve the murders. "What are we missing?"

Nate stared at him like he was crazy. "There hasn't been any evidence left behind and the cell phone was a burner with an empty sim card. The water damaged any evidence. It's not like we aren't finding things. The evidence just isn't there, Rafe. The guys are doing the best they can."

"Jenna said her tenant hasn't returned to his cabin yet. He's been gone over a week now. Our guys haven't found a trace of him. No one knew him. And he didn't talk to anyone at a neighboring cabin either." Rafe stared at the war board. He had to be missing a major piece of information, but he just couldn't see it. "Oh, by the way, I called Destiny and asked a few questions about the tissue testing she does. I asked if she had time to come back here so we can discuss it. She'll get back with me shortly to give me some dates to come back."

"Great. Hopefully she can give us some insight. The coroner should have found something on the bodies he's looked at."

"I called him this morning and got his voice mail. I'll have to wait until he calls me back. We've had pack members scouring the woods for evidence and none of them have seen anyone out there." Rafe clenched his teeth. "The damn media is waiting for me to make another statement. The public has to be on the look-out for anything suspicious. They *must* pay attention to what's going on around them."

Nate shook his head. "With summer here and more tourists, that isn't going to be easy. There are so many strangers in town, who knows if someone is acting weird or one goes missing. We can only hope that a hiker might run across a body and call us."

Rafe laughed. "Speaking of acting strange, how is Morgan doing? Because *you've* been acting strange."

He scrubbed his face and stared back at Rafe. "The need to mate is a strange thing. She has no idea what a shifter is, or the damage we can do when we mate if we aren't careful."

"That's a tough one. Should Kinsley bring it up to her? And...do you want to be around when she does?"

Nate stood up, shaking his head. He rolled his broad shoulders and stretched. "No. I'm going to her place for dinner tonight. I need to tell her about it, explain when a shift happens, before things go too far, and I just take her without thinking. That will scare her more. She's had enough assholes in her life."

Rafe checked his watch. "I'm meeting Kinsley for dinner, too. Enjoy your evening. Get going. You're off early. Relax tonight." Rafe laughed.

Nate didn't waste time getting out to his truck. Rafe hoped their evening of discussion went well.

* * * * *

Nate arrived at Morgan's apartment as planned with ribeye steaks in hand and a six pack of dark beer. She put them in the fridge. Just being near her made his urges notch up. He leaned his hip against the edge of the counter and watched her as she washed off the potatoes. Her long dark hair trailed down her slender back where her firm ass took over, sending his thoughts on a path he shouldn't go down just yet. He'd wanted her since the day they met at Suzy's Antique store. When she peeked over her shoulder, she cleared her throat to get his attention and had to drag his gaze from her firm ass to her eyes. "Just enjoying the view and got very distracted!"

"I'm glad you enjoy the view. My view isn't so bad either. I love you in a tight tee shirt. Those biceps are a bit too big for the sleeves though, but I like it that way."

"I guess I'll soon figure out all the ways you like it."

Her cheeks pinkened as she turned away. "I like it lots of ways. I can't have you getting bored on me."

Nate couldn't resist teasing her. He stepped closer, wrapped his arms around her waist and pressed himself against her ass as he nuzzled her neck. His legs locked hers between his. Her warm skin felt like satin against his lips. Even her neck tasted of strawberries. She shivered within his embrace. "I can't wait to taste you everywhere."

With that, she turned in his arms and her wet hands took his face as she kissed him. Her tongue sought his, and he let her explore as a moan slipped from her throat. He gripped her ass with one hand while his other fisted in her dark hair and gently twisted, pulling her from the kiss. He stared into those blue eyes of hers to see the pupils larger, telling him she was ready for what he wanted to show her.

Nate gently bit her lower lip, then kissed her hard as his feet stood outside of hers, trapping her between him and the cabinets. This woman turned his insides into molten lava and heated every part of his anatomy. He gripped her waist and set her on the counter. His fingers grabbed the bottom of her tank top and lifted it over her head. Her breasts lay nestled in a lace bra, her cleavage begging for his mouth. Boldly, he lifted a firm mound from the lace, exposing the hardened nipple. He took it between his lips and gently bit until she moaned, arching her back at the same time. Her breathing came faster as his thumb pressed against the center of the jeans between her thighs, rubbing her hard to test the waters.

Morgan tipped her head back as her fingers fisted in his tee shirt. "Nate...I need you bad. I can't hide it anymore. It's been so long for me. This isn't fair."

He watched her, eyes closed, head tipped back, one full breast popped out of her bra. Boldly, he took her hand and pressed it against the full length of his hardness. "It's been a while for me, too, babe."

She boldly wrapped her legs around his waist and her arms around his neck. "My room is at the end of the hall."

Nate needed no further invitation as he gripped her ass and carried her to the bed, the heat of her center resting against his own. "This isn't how I envisioned our evening going."

Morgan stared into his eyes, and he saw her need. "I did, so stop worrying."

He laughed. A bit shocked that she was moving faster than he'd planned, but he'd let her take the lead and see where this went. It'd been too long since he let the protection around his heart open the gates. "You planned to seduce me this early tonight? You're good, baby!"

In her room, Nate gently let her feet down and unhooked her bra. He took in a deep breath as he carefully freed both breasts and tossed her bra aside. As he took in the curves of her body, he breathed in her scent, exciting the wolf within. "God, Morgan. You're more beautiful than I let my mind imagine." He took her face in his hands and tenderly kissed her before they continued.

Her fingers wrapped around his forearms, then she leaned back to look up at him. "I'm yours, Nate. I've thought about this long enough."

"You have no idea what you're agreeing to. As shifters, we mate for life. Sex and mating are two different things. For me, tonight, this is *not* just sex, Morgan, and you need to understand that."

The last thing he wanted was for him to commit and this be another one-sided relationship. His heart couldn't take losing another love.

Her eyes watched him as she nodded her agreement. "I'm ready to be mated with you, Nate. I'm not sure how I know, but I do. I've been alone for five years and I know when my heart is ready. I'm ready."

His jeans tightened to nearly unbearable as her eyes nearly pleaded with him to rip her clothes off. "You need to understand that there is a chance I could shift in mid act. I don't want that to scare you, but you need to be aware that this is a possibility. You'll be mating with a wolf."

"I don't care. I'll have to see it sooner or later, correct? I did see you shift from wolf to human when you were injured on the rocks. I understand a little."

His mouth touched her lips. She pushed his senses over the edge as he hugged her closer and kissed her deeply, their tongues melding together, their breathing ragged together. Her needs nearly matched his own.

Warm fingers slipped into the waist of his jeans at the front. The button undone and the zipper slowly moved down. When his jeans were tugged and lowered, warm fingers searched inside of his underwear. They soon curled around his hardness, tight. He couldn't stop the groan that escaped as he tipped his head back when his jeans slid down his ass.

Before he realized it, warm lips covered him and the suction about undid all of his composure. Nate knotted his fingers in her hair and pulled her away, unable to even speak at that point as he tried to control the claws poking through his fingertips.

"Morgan...." Nate held her tight, unable to say more right now. Moments later, he laid her back on the bed as he knelt on the mattress between her knees and held each of her wrists over her head. His gaze moved over her body and down to her jeans as she lifted her hips to squirm beneath him. He'd strip her naked in a heartbeat if he wasn't careful. "Give me a second, woman. Damn!"

Breathe deep. Get control of yourself. You're not a young kid!

He blew out a breath as his heart slowed. When he was able to retract his claws, Nate took in another deep breath. As he stood, he reached to undo her jeans. She lay still, waiting for his next move. Once the zipper was down, his thumbs tugged the jeans over her hips and down her legs as he admired the matching lace thong. *How could I get so lucky to fall in love with a woman this sexy?* Nate tossed her jeans aside and knelt at her knees as his thumbs teased at the inner edge of the lace.

He breathed in her scent again and groaned. Unable to resist, he raised and spread her knees. His nose pressed against the lace while one hand reached for a breast, his fingers tweaking a nipple. The scent she emitted drove his wolf to the edge.

She screamed when his claws poked her nipple. "Nate!"

He realized what he'd done and immediately moved his fingers away from her. "Are you hurt? I didn't mean to lose control, but you make me crazy, woman."

Morgan met his gaze with need he couldn't believe. "I want you, babe, now. My body needs you."

Nate sat still for a moment to get his inner wolf under control. "Give me a minute. I just don't want to move this fast with you. I want to remember every inch of your body, but my wolf wants you now."

She lay silent for a moment as he breathed in.

"Let your wolf take over, babe. We can enjoy the second go-around later. I just need you inside of me, please?"

Her begging sent him over the cliff. His claws ripped away her thong and tossed his jeans aside as he mounted her, trying ever so hard to be gentle, but when she lifted her knees, he sank deep...deeper and he felt her claws trail down the muscles of his back. His hands cupped her ass, keeping her close as he moved within her. Tight inner muscles clamped around him, and his head came up as he howled for release.

Warm lips touched his neck, and her tongue trailed down to his collarbone. Her hands spread over his lower back as her legs tightened.

Nate struggled to fight off shifting as he pounded into his mate. She kept pace with him, and before he realized it, Morgan had pushed him onto his back, sat up, and rode him hard. Her eyes were black with desire and her fingers tweaked both of his nipples, sending ripples of desire directly to hardness. When she twisted, he howled again and couldn't stop the claws that appeared. He flexed his fingers so he didn't dig into her thighs. The need to touch her overwhelmed him, and he prayed the next time they mated, he'd be more in control.

Morgan closed her eyes, arched her back and met his every push with a moan. Her long dark hair floated around her like a goddess as she came to lay on his chest. Her kisses were demanding, and he accepted them. She squirmed in his arms and when he couldn't take it any longer, he felt his warm seed fill her. His woman didn't stop and kept pace for both of them before laying still on his chest.

When her breathing slowed, she slid to his side within his arms. They breathed together for several minutes; no words necessary between them. Fingers moved over his chest, and he looked down at her soft smile.

"You mate pretty good, shifter." She placed a kiss on his chest.

"I had to keep up with a woman bent on taking me."

She winked. "Don't *even* think you're close to being done yet!"

Chapter 17

Two hours later, Morgan nuzzled close to Nate's neck as his strong arms held her tight. Never had she been made to feel so special when a man had made love to her...two or three times in one session! Her ex had never made her experience what Nate had just made her feel.

She ran her fingers over the wolf tattoo on his shoulder and trailed a finger over it where the ink spread over his chest. "I hope you know how special that was for me. You made me experience feelings I've never felt before. I've never reached the stars and stayed there. Thank you." She leaned in to suck a nipple into her mouth and ran her tongue over its hardness.

Nate's fingers were beneath her chin and brought her face up to look at him. "Then it was a true mating. It feels so natural to love you, body and soul. I love your soul. You're not disappointed? Because now you're mine by shifter law. We can make it legal if you choose." The pad of his thumb caressed her lower lip and immediately a set of sparks electrified her center. Her tongue caressed the tip of his thumb. It amazed her how easily this man sent her body into a tailspin, in a good way.

He pressed her onto her back and kissed her deep, his warm body stretching over top of hers. She moved her tongue over his as his words settled into her mind. *Was this what true love felt like? Because if so, I've never truly been in love.*

Nate leaned above her, and she watched his eyes. Two different colors, but the dark pupils took over most of the color. Love and hot desire are what she saw there. Something she'd never seen in any man's eyes. "We can talk later about making it legal. Right now, I'm just happy that I belong to you. I don't need more than that right now." She kissed him again. Her hands and fingers memorized the contours of the muscles in his back, moving down to his hips, and she spread her knees.

Before either of them thought more about it, Nate slid inside of her and she tightly clamped around him, eliciting a groan. Their rhythm moved together so naturally it was as if they'd been having sex, not mating, forever. Tears pooled in her eyes and slid into her hair.

Warm lips kissed at the tear-trail, and he whispered in her ear. "I love you, Morgan. I can't explain it, but there it is." Nate pumped into her, slowly then sped up, until her breathing couldn't keep pace, nor could he reach any deeper. When stars exploded behind her eyelids, she couldn't stop the tears of happiness, her lungs void of all air as he carried her to yet another level.

As her stars streamed in color, Nate growled into her neck as he held her tight. His breathing was also labored, and she felt as exhausted as he did. When he cupped her face, he looked from one of her eyes to the other, and his thumbs wiped away the tears. "I hope those are tears of happiness, love. I would hate to think I've hurt you."

Confused, she watched him as concern took over his eyes. "I love you, too, shifter. You could never hurt me. It was beautiful. Love makes everything wonderful with you." More kisses replaced her tears.

"You've worked me into starvation." The huskiness of his voice was music to her ears.

"I think I can fix that. Can we leave the bed long enough to eat or is it too late to bother?"

He tipped his head. "It's never too late to eat. Perhaps you can prepare dinner naked since it's just the two of us? That would make me happy!"

She gasped. "No, I can't do that. But I can leave the bra here and just put my tank top back on."

He frowned. "Fine, I'll take you however you allow me."

"You can take me anytime you like, baby."

Nate pulled them up from the bed and slapped her ass. "Be careful what you promise. I *will* collect!"

After Nate pulled on his jeans, he reached for his tee shirt and Morgan grabbed it from his hand. "I want you in just jeans." Her wink got her a smile that covered his face.

"As you wish, love." His arm snaked around her waist before she could get dressed and his hand claimed a breast. She couldn't complain because his hands on her body kept her wanting him.

"Dinner still needs to be fixed. If you don't let me go, I may have to resort to magick and just whip it up!" The words slipped out faster than she could think and then wondered if that was something she could even do. Surprised at her own words, she met his gaze.

"Would that be such a bad thing? It's not like it's against the law, right? It's just you and I here, so I say, give it a try. What could happen?" Nate kissed her nose then pulled her tank top over her head and stood back to check for visible nipples. She quickly covered them and laughed, but he pulled her hands away. "Those are mine now and I want to see them. Sorry, love."

Morgan laughed and picked up her shredded lace thong, then looked at Nate. "We can't afford to have this happen every time we mate."

Nate laughed, snatched them from her hand and stuffed them into his pocket. "I'll buy you one-hundred pair just so you don't worry in the future. For now, you don't need these with your jeans either."

She widened her eyes at his suggestion. "I've never in my life gone without underwear!"

"Today, you're commando. Sorry." He handed her jeans to her, and she slipped them on, not sure if she'd like her body fluids on her jeans!

Making her way down the hall, Morgan wondered if she could swirl her fingers and have their dinner cooked to perfection and appear on the plate. Nate had followed her to the kitchen, and she glanced at him, then at their pre-seasoned steaks and the potatoes she'd planned to bake.

"Give it a swirl of your magick fingers and see what happens. It'll be our little secret."

"Okay, here goes." Morgan closed her eyes, concentrated on the end result of a grilled steak and baked potato, then gave a slight swirl of her fingers. Before she could open her eyes, the smell of a freshly grilled steak wafted to her senses and her eyes flew open, still amazed that she had abilities. "Holy shit, Nate!" There on the plates rested each steak, steaming, and the potatoes, baked and sliced open with sour cream and bacon bits.

When she looked at him, his eyes were as wide as hers. He opened his arms, and she stepped into them for a huge hug. "I do love my little witch and her magick. Should we eat before they get cold? Do you prefer beer or a wine?" Nate opened the fridge.

"A beer, please." She leaned toward him for a kiss then got silverware and steak knives out. Nate handed her a beer and they went to sit by the television to eat. Once she got settled, Morgan cut into her steak, hoping it would be perfect, even with using magick. She wasn't disappointed, but she was shocked. "Oh, my goddess, this is delicious!"

Nate had cut into his and nodded his approval. Eating didn't leave much time for conversation, but once they were finished, they both got a fresh beer and cuddled on the sofa. She leaned against him with her head on his shoulder, loving the feel of skin to skin. "I don't ever recall being this happy before. Is that bad? I have a beautiful son, but I can't say I was ever in love before today."

"You have filled a void in my life, too. My heart is full today, Morgan. I've never told another woman that." She glanced up at him and he kissed her. "I'm honored that I am the one to make you feel loved. You are so precious to me." He trailed a finger down her shoulder and just his slight touch sent her mind back to her bedroom.

"What are we going to tell everyone? What is Rafe going to say?" She wasn't sure her coven would be happy that she and Nate had found happiness.

"Rafe will be the first one to congratulate us. I promise. He'll give me shit and have fun doing it, but I don't care. If both of us are happy in our new relationship, we won't care what others think. Unless...your son won't be happy."

Morgan hadn't thought about Logan or what he thought of Nate. She hoped he wouldn't accuse her of jumping into bed with the first man she met. After all, she'd been divorced for over five years now. But Nate was the first man she'd thought about like that. There hadn't even been other dates before Nate. She just hadn't been interested. "When he sees how happy you make me, he won't say a word. How can he?"

"I won't let him down. Your happiness is my first priority."

"No, your job is your first priority. We will work around everything and figure out where we go from here. We have a wonderful future ahead of us."

Nate's phone dinged as a message came in, and he checked it. "It's Rafe. Let me see what he wants. He never sends a text this late. Let's hope it's not another body." After reading, Nate let out a laugh and glanced at her. "He wants to know if my wolf was successful tonight!"

"Don't you tell him a thing!" Her cheeks heated and then her neck. "Is that what guys talk about?"

His laughter rang out. "No, we don't. But he did wish me luck as I left the station earlier tonight. I'll just send him a smiley face!"

She punched his shoulder and laughed with him. "Now Kinsley will know, too. We'll be talked about by everyone. We won't have to tell them. They'll know!" Morgan leaned back against the sofa and stared at the ceiling. At least she was finally in love, and nothing mattered from here on out. Nate would always be at her side.

Nate had never been happier than he was tonight as he admired his new mate. Taking her had been better than he could ever have imagined, other than his wolf escaping on more than one occasion, but Morgan seemed to be okay with it all. Now he didn't want to leave. He didn't want to let her out of his sight.

Thoughts of the demon came into mind. How could he protect her when he didn't possess magick of his own. He'd be powerless against the demon. Perhaps Kinsley would know how to proceed. They would have to meet with her and Rafe, but not tonight.

"I don't want to leave you tonight and go back to an empty bed." Would she agree?

Morgan met his gaze. "Then stay here tonight. Set your alarm so you aren't late for work and give yourself enough time to be home and change."

His heart swelled even more that she was on the same thought as he was. He reached for her and pulled her close as they finished their beers. "At some point, I want you to decide that you'll move into my place, but it needs a woman's touch. Would you miss not living in this tiny apartment?"

Her pause gave him worry as she thought about what he'd said. "I would love to move into your home. I'm not sure how you've not gotten lost in a house so large, from what you said about it."

"It's been lonely, and I spend more time at the station so I don't have to roam around there wondering who would fill it with me. Now I won't have to anymore." Nate smiled, happy to know she would fill his home with love. It'd been empty for far too long.

* * * * *

The next evening, Morgan walked on the beach hand in hand with Nate. The crickets chirped near the woods. She loved the feeling of warm sand in her toes, and standing at the edge of the water as the waves cooled her feet. Nate held her hand with their fingers entwined. Tonight, he walked barefoot in his jeans as though he didn't care that the water soaked the bottoms. The sun still shown, and he had his shirt off, tucked in the back pocket of his pants to get some sun. His tan was already dark, and she admired the way his muscles moved over his back and chest.

Even before they mated, his interest was uncharted as she knew it. Never in her life had anyone paid her this much attention. He texted her daily if he didn't call or show up at her apartment.

Nate tugged her close as they stood in the small waves and kissed her. "I love seeing you smile." His thumb tenderly caressed her cheek.

"All because of you. You've brought sunshine into my life, yet I don't know much about you. I know you're single and live alone with no women coming in and out of your life. I have to ask. Did something happen in your past with a woman that made you not want one around?" Morgan wondered what could have happened to make a man not want companionship for so long. She watched him closely for any sign she may have missed.

He met her eyes, but there was no smile on his lips. "I don't mean to keep things from you. Please don't take it that way." Nate paused and shook sand off his foot in the water. "I was mated fifteen years ago. She was beautiful and we were very happy, maybe too happy. I'm not sure we're allowed to be happy in this life because then shit happens."

"I'm sorry you had to go through whatever it was that destroyed your outlook."

He glanced down at her, a moment of silence. "A car accident shattered my life. I wasn't with her when it happened. A drunk driver crossed the center line. There weren't even skid marks from her tires, so she had no reaction time when the head-on collision happened." Nate squeezed her fingers and took in a breath. His eyes pooled with unshed tears. "I pray I never have to go through that again. One worries daily if their life will be shattered by the wrong of another. I don't ever want to lose you now that we've found happiness for both of us."

Nate's arms wrapped around her, and she held him tight, his muscles knotting beneath her fingers. Her heart ached for him and what he must have gone through. Sometimes things happen that we can't control, and she knew that well enough.

"Well, well, isn't this just a happy union!"

Immediately, Morgan's happiness shattered into a million pieces as she recognized that voice. Her muscles tightened with panic. When she opened her eyes, Dantalion sat atop of the nearby rocks that jutted from the shoreline. If she hadn't hated him so much, the man could almost be sexy with his longer curly hair, but the evil that emanated from his soul could never be denied.

Nate spun around and kept Morgan behind him. "You! Morgan doesn't need your kind around. What do you want from her? It's obvious you made some deadly deal with her mother. Go back and find *her*!"

"And you are just a rude asshole, my friend. I've not wronged anyone here so why the anger toward me?" Dantalion tipped his head and smiled as he waved a hand over the water and toward the shoreline.

A ten-foot wave rose up and covered Morgan and Nate, knocking them both ashore into the sand, soaking them. She coughed up water and before she could recover, another huge wave swept ashore. When it receded, something dragged Nate by the feet into the waves. As he tried to shake off whatever it was, he ended up in deeper water and then went under.

Morgan screamed as she scrambled to her feet and trudged out to where Nate had gone under, digging at the water in search of him. When laughter rang out over the water from the rocks, she turned toward Dantalion, screaming at him to bring Nate back.

"He is not whom you belong to. I'm sorry you see it that way. You were promised to me years ago, and I tire of waiting." The demon jumped from the rocks and stood on the sand in jeans and a tee shirt. Gone was his business suit from the other day.

Splashing sounded behind Morgan when suddenly a huge wolf leapt from the water and bounded toward Dantalion so fast she only saw a blue streak of light. The wolf jumped at the demon and sank its teeth into Dantalion's neck as they both landed in the sand. The wolf shook its head, teeth tight around the neck, and the pair rolled several times.

Right before her eyes, Dantalion disappeared and the wolf turned toward her, confused, blood dripping from his jaws. The wolf raced toward her and into the water, rinsing the evidence away. Watching this right in front of her, Morgan saw Nate shift back to human form as his jeans floated atop the next wave that came ashore.

She made her way to the sandy beach, her gaze looking everywhere for the demon to reappear in the tree line or back on the rocks. He was nowhere, yet she searched twice again. Nate had stayed in the water as he slid back into his jeans, then ran ashore to be with her. "I don't understand what all that was about, Nate. What does he want?"

"I would think your mom can answer that." He took her shoulders and turned her around. "Are you hurt? I should have known better to bring you down to the beach. There aren't any wards down here to protect you from him."

"It's not your fault, babe. I'm fine, just a bit shaky. He tried to kill you!" Every fiber inside of her ignited sparks as Morgan thought about how close she came to losing Nate. *At the whim of a demon!* She knew she had to reach out to her mother and demand answers. *What the hell kind of deal had her parents made that promised her to a damn demon?*

Morgan took hold of Nate's cold hands. "Hang on, hon. Close your eyes and trust me." She concentrated on her living room, felt the electricity spread through her body and soon they both stood in her apartment. Opening her eyes, she looked around to be sure they were alone and Dantalion hadn't somehow hitched a ride. "We should be safe from him here since I've warded the building from him. I have so many questions for my parents!"

"You're getting the hang of those magickal powers of yours. I kind of like this!" Nate took her face in his hands to calm her down and made her look at him. "We'll get this figured out. I won't let anyone come between us." His mouth took hers, and she held him tight as his love for her seeped into her body.

Placing her forehead on his chest, Morgan tried to make sense of what had just happened. Her fingers sought the *tree of life* necklace, held it tight in her fingers, and concentrated on her mother. "I need you *right now*! What have you done?"

Nate held her at arm's length, her eyes closed as she spoke out loud. When she opened them, she kept the necklace in her fingers. Her cell phone rang. "That better be her!" She grabbed her cell phone and answered. "Mom?"

"Morgan, I'm so sorry. I just saw the vision of what happened. Stay put. Your father and I will be there in a few minutes. We need to talk." The line went dead.

She stared at Nate. "I'm assuming they're both teleporting here in a few minutes. What kind of deal could they possibly have made that gave me to a demon?" Morgan paced and went into the kitchen. She wanted a beer or wine, but now wasn't the time. A clear head is what she needed to make sense of all this. "Should I call Kinsley? Does she need to know since I think she's aware of who this demon is?"

"I'll text Rafe. He'll know what to do. I'm glad we left our cell phones here and didn't take them to the beach with us! They'd be ruined." He sent a text and within minutes, he got an answer back. "Rafe and Kinsley are on their way here. I told them to meet us at the back door of the store rather than up here. When your parents arrive, bring them downstairs." He reached for her and held her trembling body.

Just his touch gave her a sense of security. She didn't want to be alone even for a minute, but he would let Rafe and Kinsley in. "Be careful down there. The wards are in place, so the demon can't get inside to us. I'll be down soon." She stood on her toes and kissed him before he left. "I love you." Her fingers trailed over his jaw as she realized the how much she did love him.

"Love you, too, baby. Lock this behind me." Nate headed down to watch for Rafe and Kinsley.

Chapter 18

Nate unlocked the door when he saw Rafe through the peephole, then locked the door once they were inside. Relief is the only word that came to mind when his friends walked in. He didn't know how to fight a demon since his wolf couldn't hold onto it! What good was he? He needed to know how to protect her from this.

"Well, this isn't how I expected to find you. I could have brought you a shirt." Rafe sniffed the air. "You mated her, didn't you?"

Nate gave him a sideways glance and moved into the bookstore with them following. He pulled chairs out in the cafe area and sat at a table. Leaning back in his chair, he stared at Rafe, then glanced at Kinsley and back. "Yes...we did. We are."

Rafe held out his hand and Nate shook it. "You deserve to be happy again. I can see you are. It suits you. Now, tell us what happened tonight."

After a long explanation, Kinsley sat wide-eyed. "That bastard! He has no right to be here. He tried to kill you, Nate!"

"Obviously her parents made some sort of deal for their firstborn, and he's here to collect!"

"There has to be a way to fight him. I've made my own deals with him years ago. He doesn't go away."

Nate looked up when Morgan walked in with her parents. She had a smile on her face and a shirt for him in her hand. "I thought you might need this. Not that I want you covered up, but my mother doesn't need to see more than she already has."

He laughed and took the shirt, quickly pulling it on over his head, tugging it down his abs, his fingers smoothing the material. "Better?"

She met his gaze and rolled her eyes. "No, but for the time being, it'll have to work." She sat down next to him, and he put his hand on her thigh as her parents dragged chairs over. Morgan made the introductions, for her parents again, to Kinsley and Rafe, and himself. He just couldn't get a read on her father nor his expression.

Does he approve of her being with a wolf?

"Thanks for coming over so late tonight. I need to know what's happening and *why*!" Morgan rested her elbows on the table and tapped her fingers together, obviously nervous.

Her father stared down his nose at Nate as he moved in his chair as though he were under a microscope. "You're a shifter. You *do* realize what a relationship with my daughter means for any children?"

"Dad! I don't plan on any more children."

A raised brow was his only answer. "You've *mated* with him." His eyes went from her to Nate and back.

"That isn't up for discussion tonight. This demon friend of yours is what we're here for." Morgan knew she had to keep her anger under control or the space around her would electrify. She'd learned that much.

"We all know he's no one's friend." Her father set his jawline.

Morgan splayed her fingers over the tabletop as she leaned toward her father. "Yet, it seems you gave me away to him before I was old enough to understand any of it. What's up with that, *dad*?"

He closed his eyes and sighed, then looked at his wife. "The reason is not important. The council will never allow that to happen. I'll keep you both posted when I hear back from the Aether with a plan."

"And that's it? I don't need to understand any of it? I know nothing about this *witch's council,* yet I understand they are all powerful, and we must abide by their laws as coven members."

Her father's brows rose. "Morgan! I've never before done anything to make you distrust me. Please don't start now. In the meantime, please try not to move around town alone."

Nate looked directly at her father. "Who is this guy and what deal was made so long ago that he feels Morgan belongs to him? Because she doesn't. She belongs to *me* now. I'll do everything in my power to protect her from him. He needs to understand that."

"Son, it's not so cut and dry. Dantalion was a warlock. He's over two-hundred years old. He went to the dark side one-hundred years ago and spent time in jail of the witch's council for being a part of the dark demonic side."

"So, that makes you two over one-hundred years old?" Nate looked between them and over at Morgan, who appeared just as shook up as all of them.

Kinsley leaned on the table. "So how did he escape jail at the witch's council? I understand that isn't an easy feat."

Her father appeared wise beyond his years. His dark hair was neatly combed, not a hair out of place. Nate would never have guessed at his true age. "Trickery...and magick. He was a powerful warlock and when he flipped, he got even more powerful with every witch or warlock he stole powers from and then killed, which is against coven law. The witch's council is now aware of him and what he's up to...again. The Aether is working on it. He's meeting with the council and will get back to me as to what their decision will be. They have ways of re-arresting him and getting him back behind bars...magickal bars that he can't escape from again. He knew there were restrictions should he ever escape, and he's ignored those, which gives them the right to get him back into their custody. We just don't know how long that might take."

Rafe tipped his head and looked down his nose at her father. Nate stiffened, not sure what the leader of their pack would say now. "It's my responsibility to protect our witches in this community. My pack spans three of our villages and they have all pledged protection. So, your daughter is safe among us. We just don't know how to get rid of this demon."

"He's a bit more powerful than any of your witches." Morgan's mother stroked the amulet she wore. "I felt the wards on this building. That will keep him out only for so long. Please be sure those are redone every thirty days to keep the wards active." She gave Morgan a worried glance and Nate slipped his arm around his mate's shoulder.

Kinsley reassured her. "We have put the wards in place on several of our coven businesses to keep him out. We just need to be aware when we are out around town. Our herbs and basil water were replenished to re-ward each business."

Annette nodded. Her husband reached out to take her hand and she squeezed it. Nate wondered what secret they were keeping since they had not yet explained the issue and Morgan hadn't pressed them for an answer yet. It wasn't his place to do so, but very hard to sit and not say a word. This wasn't how he wanted to start their relationship.

Her father stood, as did her mother. "We will leave you two alone. I'll call when I hear what the plan is. I promise. Please be careful." He reached a hand to Nate. "Please keep her safe for us."

With hesitation, Nate shook his hand. "Yes, sir."

Within seconds, electricity sparked the air and the two disappeared. Morgan just shook her head.

He brushed her hair away from her face and tipped her face up. "We'll figure this out, babe. You aren't alone here." His heart felt near bursting in his chest with finally finding a love to surpass all others. He knew she was right for him.

"Can we be the first to congratulate both of you?" Kinsley stood and came over to Morgan. "You are one lucky woman, Morgan! I can already see how happy you are."

Morgan hugged her back. Her blush moved up her neck to her cheeks. "I truly am. Thank you."

Morgan took the hand Nate reached over to her, and she met his gaze. Her smile reached her eyes, and he knew how lucky his heart was. With so many incidents happening tonight, he wanted to get her back upstairs.

Kinsley looked at Rafe. "Should we pop back over to my place and celebrate?"

Rafe raised a brow at Nate. "Well?"

Morgan answered for them. "I think that's a great idea."

Nate squeezed her hand and pulled her close. "Then, later, we'll return to your place, Morgan. I don't want to take a chance on you being at my house until we can get a ward up there to protect you."

"I can make that happen with Angela's help. We'll get on that tomorrow. Let's go." Kinsley seemed excited for them, and Nate kissed Morgan's cheek.

"We'll be right there. I'll shut off the lights and head up to lock my apartment." Morgan didn't let go of Nate's hand. Rafe and Kinsley disappeared, and once back in Morgan's apartment, he made sure her door was locked and deadbolted.

Nate reached out for Morgan before she could head to the kitchen. He pulled her against him, just wanting to hold her for a moment and kissed the top of her head. "I want you safe. I'd drive over to Kinsley's place, but I think your magickal way is safer for us tonight."

She leaned back and looked up at him. Her thumb caressed his lower lip and sent a spark straight down to his center. His tongue slipped out to wet her thumb. "We can delay our arrival if you wish."

He felt a shiver run through her body as she thought it over. "We can save that thought for when we return. How's that?"

"If you insist." A chuckle rumbled in his chest as he dropped a kiss on her warm lips, instantly tasting her.

She took his hand. "Are you ready? We're doing this only for safety reasons and because no one will see us."

Nate felt the sparking magick as Morgan closed her eyes and envisioned Kinsley's home. When he opened his own eyes, they stood in the screened porch as the magick traveled out of his fingertips from his mate. He didn't think he'd ever get over the unrealistic possibilities of what she could do once she learned everything. Their future could be filled with lots of unknown happenings.

Morgan shook the magickal sparks out her hands as they stood in the screened room at Kinsley's. *Would she ever get used to being able to teleport anywhere? Why now when she could have made good use of her abilities so many years ago?* Maybe the answers were in the grimoire. She looked up at Nate and took his hand again. "Let's go inside. We have some celebrating to do. Thank you for being so special!"

Nate took her hand and kissed the back of it.

Rafe appeared in the doorway as Morgan glanced up. "I thought I heard something out here. Come on! Kinsley is waiting for the toast. Everyone, the guests of honor have arrived!"

Nate accepted a beer from Rafe, and Morgan took a glass of Riesling from Angela, who joined their group. "Thank you. Good to see you, Angela. And thank you again for the wards at my store. We need to ward Nate's home next."

Kinsley held up her glass with Angela, and Morgan joined them. "Wishes for years of happiness to the new couple!"

Morgan's neck heated and it moved up to her cheeks. She was happy, finally. "Thank you."

Nate stepped closer and cupped the back of her head as he pulled her in for a kiss. She didn't resist. It felt so normal, even in front of her friends. The warmth that his kiss sent through her made her insides burn with need and she couldn't wait to get home later.

Their friends cheered, and Nate released her to join in the toast. She hoped life would always feel this happy. They sat around the table and talked of what might be done about the demon. Morgan thanked Angela for her willingness to get more herbs and water ready to ward Nate's home so she would be protected there.

Nate squeezed his beer can and dented it. "I hate that we don't know his reasoning nor where he'll show up next. At least we can feel his presence when he's around, but it's usually too late when we sense him. Like the other day in your store when he approached your mom."

"But neither of us sensed him at the beach." Morgan looked at Kinsley. "His wolf's teeth drew blood on the demon's neck. I doubt that did any actual damage though."

Kinsley shook her head. "No. He would heal immediately with his abilities. I hope the Aether has an idea that will work. We can only wait and see."

Morgan's heart twisted with a need to know why her parents would make such a deal. At least her friends were aware. A fix had to happen.

An hour later, she and Nate returned to her apartment where she felt safer. Just when she thought her life would be better, it wasn't. Like Nate had said, when one is happy, shit happens. She would have to keep her own senses sharp when she was out and about town.

* * * * *

Tonight, the clouds covered the moon, making it black on the lonely highway. No other cars followed, nor came from up ahead.

Thirty-five minutes had passed slowly as the pick-up sped through the night. Taking a turn into the woods, the rarely used road was familiar as the headlights guided the way.

Bumps.

Sharp turns.

Treacherous roadways.

Deeper into the trees where no humans traveled, the driver's sweaty hands slipped on the steering wheel before the truck came to a stop. The driver grabbed the headband with a work light and slipped it on, then turned it on.

The knives rested in the leg pocket of the cargo pants.

The tailgate opened without a sound and the body bag fell over the edge onto the ground with a grunt. A hand reached into the opening in search of a pulse.

Still strong.

Good tranquilizers.

With renewed vigor, the driver grabbed the large cooler and dragged the body over the ferns that covered the forest floor until they reached the proper location...at the edge of the ravine.

No sign of others in the area as the light shined through the darkness.

Damp, earthy scents permeated the area.

The bag is unzipped, the body rolled out, and the bag tossed away to avoid getting any of the victim's blood spatter on it. Straddling the body, fingers and thumbs press the throat and prepare for a slight struggle.

In time.

Limbs flail, the body jerks, then stops moments later.

No movement.

One more long squeeze and a snap.

Thankful for past training, the driver pulls out the knives and rubber gloves, and the cooler is pulled closer, open and ready. The victim's clothing is torn open, fingers slip into the gloves and the sharp blade sparkles against the headlamp.

Deep, even cuts, but careful not to slice into organs.

Precious parts that help others have a new life.

Two kidneys. Two lungs. A heart.

Extra arteries.

No one will miss the male.

This is for you, mother.

The correct arteries are cut, organs slipped into separate bags, into the cooler among the ice packs, until each bag is filled.

The lid of the cooler protects the bags nestled among the ice packs.

Knives are wrapped and replaced in the pocket.

The body is rolled to the edge and pushed over into the ravine. The carcass rolls gently to the bottom among more ferns.

Gloves dropped into another bag and taken back to the truck with the body bag, into the passenger side. The truck makes its way back to the main road.

The dealer awaits the cooler.

Money will be mine.

Mother would be proud.

Another fifteen minutes and the side road eventually lead to the shoreline. The front of the boat is in the sand, the driver waiting. With the truck lights left on, the cooler is rushed to the boat and handed over.

The envelope is within grasp.

"I shouldn't even pay you. You are going to get both of us arrested or worse!"

Fingers tightened on the handle of the cooler, not willing to release it until the envelope lands in the other hand.

A paper cut!

The cooler is released as the fingers tighten on the money transfer.

"I'll be in touch."

The bow is pushed away from the sand and the boat floats out farther before the engine is started. Back in the truck, the darkness swallows the boat as it disappears. Turning toward the road, the truck speeds down the dark highway, elation rises as fingers smooth over the steering wheel, except for the finger with the papercut.

More cash for the box.

Each time gets easier.

Another life or two will be saved, maybe three.

Too bad mother never got that chance.

Chapter 19

The next morning, Morgan heard Nate's alarm. The mattress dipped as he got up, shut it off, then joined her beneath the covers again. She rolled toward him as he scooped her hip to pull her close. His hardness pressed against her as her fingers trailed over his jaw. He took her mouth with a passion that ignited her need all over again as their tongues melded...just as he took the rest of her body, and she loved it. Rolling onto her back, he slid between her knees and thrust up inside of her, making Morgan gasp and moan. When she pulled her knees up, he thrust deeper, and she matched his pace.

Thirty minutes later, she still didn't want Nate to leave as he held her close, their heads on the pillow. His eyes pulled her in as easily as his arms did. He seemed to know exactly how she needed him to touch her, and she couldn't get enough. "You're just trying to get me addicted, aren't you?"

He gave her a crooked smile. "Is it working?"

She couldn't resist running her thumb over his lower lip. "It must be. Who mates this often over a two-day period?"

"Shifters. I can't have you getting bored on me. But I do need to hit the shower before I head home to change. Be right back, babe." She admired the muscles of his ass as he tossed the covers and strode to the bathroom, appearing too comfortable being naked.

Morgan heard the shower, and she rolled onto her side of the bed to get up. She pulled on her light blue silk robe and tied it, then walked to the kitchen to get the coffee going. He should at least have a good cup of joe as he drove home. Living with Nate at his home would be different. Could she leave her small apartment? Maybe Logan would want it if she decided to move in with Nate. She'd keep that in mind.

Once the coffee started dripping through, she dug around for a travel mug for Nate. Standing on her tip toes to reach the top shelf, his hand beat her to it as another snaked around her waist and pulled her against a warm chest.

As he set the mug on the counter, his nose pressed into her hair, and he breathed in. "God, I could hold you all day and smell that. How do you smell like strawberries?"

She tipped her head back onto his shoulder and he nibbled her neck. When a warm tongue moved over her skin, her knees nearly buckled. A man had never made her feel what he does, and she closed her eyes to enjoy everything he did to her senses.

"I love that you're putty in my hands."

A gasp tore from her throat and then a laugh. "Don't overestimate yourself, hon. I can be strong!"

"I know you can. You're a great role model for other women, but it's not other women I want."

She turned in his arms and touched her lips to his. "This is all a bit overwhelming, but I love what you make me feel. I can get used to this."

"I hope when we get you moved into my place, that you'll still feel that way. As much as I want to hang around, I do need to get to the station."

She added creamer to both cups and filled them, then put the lid on his.

Nate tasted it and met her gaze. "Almost as good as you taste. What are your plans for today? I'll call you later when I can."

"It's early so I might enjoy my coffee as I read the family grimoire some more. I hope I can take it all in and learn some of my history." She followed him to the door and gave him a key. He looked confused. "It's for the deadbolt downstairs on the backdoor."

"I'll lock you in, babe. Have a great day." Nate slipped out and she turned the deadbolt and leaned against the door.

Never had she ever had her head in the clouds because of her feelings. Nate was definitely a different sort of man. Morgan got comfortable on the sofa and pulled the family book onto her lap. The parchment pages contained such a wealth of information. She moved to the marker that had been put in place the last time she read. The next few pages contained notes on how to bless a space for rituals and the candles that needed to be used along with sage. Those items would be easy to obtain.

Would Nate's home have a room that she could use for her herbs and candles...and spells? Would she actually be doing these kinds of things as a witch? She was anxious to see his home and how large it was. He'd told her it was off the main road, and he could see the ocean from his back porch. That sounded peaceful.

Reading through some of the rituals, Morgan knew she would need to reread them several times before she felt confident enough to use them for good. Turning the pages, she scanned for information on the family warlock history and where it would place Logan. The writing was at least a hundred years old, and some areas were hard to read but the explanations made sense. Decades ago, it stated that the first-born son of every other generation would be chosen to be a powerful warlock, to lead his witches and warlocks against all evil. Their powers would develop in their early twenties.

Goosebumps crawled over Morgan's arms. That's exactly where Logan was right now. She needed more coffee if she were going to keep reading. Was she ready to accept the place in the witch's community Logan would hold? She tossed off the afghan, shook off the eerie feeling, and poured fresh coffee with cream.

As she walked back to the sofa, the electricity rippled, and Morgan stopped. Izzy appeared in her chair with her own cup of tea. "Good morning, my dear. I thought perhaps you might need an elder to help you wade through those pages and understand it. I felt the calling of the ancient spirits that dwell inside the book. They informed me you might need some interpretation."

Morgan got comfortable, pulled a blanket over her legs and the family book. Having Izzy appear at odd times was getting easier for her and half expected. She sipped her coffee as she listened to the old woman.

"It's a lot to take in when you aren't trained from childhood, but I have no doubt that you will learn quickly, as will your son. He is destined to be a powerful leader, and I know he will handle it like a pro." She tipped her cup to drink. "Close your eyes and let yourself concentrate on the future. You have the ability to see what is ahead of you if you just get out of your own way."

Morgan set down her coffee, then closed her eyes as her fingers splayed over the pages in front of her. Through the darkness of her vision, she could make out figures fighting with swords and flashes of lightning sparked around them. As the warriors came into better view, she could see it was Logan and Dantalion. Her son matched him in size and stature, which was not how her son was today. What happened that he would grow to be so strong and powerful? When Dantalion raised his sword above Logan's head, Morgan cried out as she pulled her hands off the book.

The vision shook Morgan to her core at seeing Logan fight Dantalion. She rubbed her temples, trying to make sense of it all. The answers had to be in the grimoire.

Remembering that Izzy was present, she glanced her way. "Is there an easy way to learn what I must so Logan is prepared for this?"

"Nothing is ever easy, my dear. But the answers *are* in the book where the family history is. There you will find how other protectors have been instructed. Your father may very well have an instructor for Logan already in mind. He's been instructed over his lifetime to know this would come to be. I will leave you to read. You know I'm just a call away should you need me."

Morgan watched her disappear, then with shaking fingers, reached for her coffee, hoping it would calm her nerves. She savored the hot creamy liquid and had to go refill her mug. Once resettled with the book on her lap, careful not to tear the old parchment pages, she located the section with family history and words about every other generation of first-born sons.

She read it again. That meant that her father was one, making Logan the next generation. Which meant Logan's grandson would also be a protector with abilities. *Exactly what abilities?* Morgan carefully turned the pages as she read, the smell of the ancient book permeating her senses. She learned that Logan would be able to sense all beings coming toward him, move earth, wind, fire, and water to protect those he loved just by concentrating on what he wanted to achieve.

The writing spoke of practicing what one wanted to accomplish with their powers, but it could only be used for protection and safety. She read of one being who got so angry that the earth split around him, and the enemies fell to their death before the cracks sealed up. Or that the need for safety would whip up a hurricane or tornado to sweep away enemies.

Morgan's phone rang, startling her from her studies. Hours had passed while she sat here learning and her head swam with new information. Nate's face appeared on her phone. "Hey, babe. What's up?"

"Logan just made me a coffee and said he hadn't seen you all day. I'm just checking to be sure you're okay."

"Oh, my goddess. I've been reading our family grimoire since you left this morning. That was hours ago." She hadn't realized how much time had passed. "Come up if you have time. I guess I better get ready for my day!"

"I'll make time, hon. Bye."

She looked around, for what, she wasn't sure. "Let's try out this magick stuff." She closed her eyes, mentally washed her face and brushed her teeth, and envisioned jeans and a tee shirt, then snapped her fingers.

Morgan screeched when she saw her clothes changed and her hair in a ponytail. A knock on the door brought her back to reality. Nate had arrived and she opened it.

His gaze raked down her body and back up. "I thought you said you hadn't cleaned up. You look ravishing."

Her face heated. "I may have cheated with a snap of my fingers."

Nate smiled, shook his head, and reached his arms out to take her. His strong hug put her into the clouds. "I know you can't stay long, but I'm glad you stopped by."

"I had a nice conversation with Logan. Told him a friend of mine was the local vet. If he were interested, I could give him a referral."

"Nate, that would be his dream job! Thank you!"

A huge smiled covered his face. "He seemed excited."

Morgan took his face in her hands and kissed him, but Nate took more than a short peck. His mouth took hers in a kiss that gave her butterflies. Before his tongue tasted hers, Morgan's knees easily buckled.

A quickie was out of the question!

He gave her a moment to catch her breath. "I can walk down with you. I have a few book orders to check over before sending them off." But the last thing she wanted to do was let go of Nate. He made her feel loved and secure.

"I'd love nothing more than to stay here the rest of the day and make you smile, but I have rounds to make before my shift is done. Let me know your plans for the evening." He gave her a quick kiss and a squeeze of her ass.

"Do you even realize how sexy you are?" She trailed a thumb over his lower lip, only to feel the bulge press against her front. "Damn, babe!"

"You create sexy thoughts in my head, but we can't stay up here. Logan knows I came to check on you. I can't have him thinking bad of me. Let's go see how he's doing."

Down at the coffee shop, Logan glanced up as Morgan and Nate walked in and then looked at his watch, making her laugh. She was proud of the man he was becoming. It was his future that concerned her.

Logan looked at her, Nate, and back at Morgan. He gave that toss of hair to get it out of his eyes and grinned at her. "Is there something I need to know?"

Morgan giggled. "What's that supposed to mean?"

"I wasn't born yesterday, mom. As long as I see you smiling, I'll keep my nose out of it." He poured chocolate raspberry into a coffee, gave it a quick stir, and handed it to her. "Did you learn more from the book?"

She took the cup and savored the smell. "I did, actually. We should get together and go over it. There's a lot there about the family protectors you need to know." Her phone vibrated in her back pocket, and she pulled it out to answer. "Hey, dad. What's up?"

"Hi, hon. I'm concerned about Logan's abilities. I think we need to jump on his training as soon as possible. He's just finding out about this, and I don't want him confused now that we know he has them."

"Sure." Morgan looked at Logan and stepped over to a table. "Hold on, dad." She covered her phone. "I have to take this, sorry."

Nate saluted her. "I'll call you later, babe."

She watched him walk out, then met Logan's smile as he shook his head at her drooling over Nate. He gave her a thumbs up and relief spread through her system. "Okay, dad. Sorry. Nate just left. So, tell me what you're thinking."

"Your mother agrees. I'd like an old friend of mine to spend a few weeks there training and working with Logan. Her name is Jadis."

"How old is this friend, dad?" Morgan imagined someone like Izzy…a bit feeble to train a twenty-two-year-old.

"Her age isn't important. She has the knowledge and skill to teach him what he needs to learn as a protector. Jadis can be there in a few days, if that works for Logan."

"That works. I'll let him know so he can be ready. Thanks, dad. Love you."

"We love you, too, hon. Talk to you soon."

Morgan tucked her phone away and enjoyed the rest of her coffee. Logan busied himself taking care of the regulars and asking them about their day. They would miss him should he go to work for the vet, but that was his passion.

He finished up and sat with her at the table. "So, Nate seems like a nice guy. Did he tell you he's going to talk with the local vet for me? I'm kind of excited."

"He did tell me. I'd hate to lose your help here but that would be a great move for you. Help me find a replacement for you before you leave."

"I don't have the job yet, mom." Logan relaxed back in his chair and looked her in the eye. "I can see Nate makes you happy, mom. I can't say I've ever seen that look in your eye when dad was around. I like the change in you. Dad was an asshole anyway."

Morgan touched Logan's hand and squeezed it. "I've never been this happy, Logan. I'm glad you like him. He wants me to move in with him when I'm ready. We have to put up wards at his home before I move there. *If* I do, this apartment can be yours if you want it."

"That's a big step, mom, but you've been unhappy for too long. Move at your own pace though. Don't rush this." He leaned over and kissed her cheek. "Now. What did gramps call about?"

Morgan watched his expression. "He has an old friend he wants you to train with, so you are prepared for your future. I think it's important." She couldn't stop her vision from repeating in her head of the sword fight. Would she have seen the end if she hadn't stopped the vision?

"It's kind of hard to wrap my head around…all this magick stuff. I don't even know what is possible, mom." He shook his head and toyed with the napkin on the table.

"I don't understand it all either, son. We'll learn together. Has Mandy shown she has abilities?" Morgan hoped the two had at least brought up the subject.

Logan twisted the napkin in his fingers. "I know her mom has abilities, so I just assumed that Mandy does too. I've not seen her use them for evil, if that's what you're asking."

"Has she done magick around you?"

He met her eyes. "Yes, just simple things, like making a glass appear. That kind of stuff."

"And were you aware that you might have abilities?"

"Mom, I didn't even know it might be possible for me to have that ability. I have to be honest. It's kind of scary to think I'm going to be singled out to be a 'protector'…whatever that might be."

Morgan touched his arm. "I didn't really understand it when I read about it today in the book. What I did understand was that your powers would be almost endless with what you could do in the way of magick. It described it like having you be so angry that you could manipulate the earth to open, and your enemies would fall to their death and then the ground would move back together like nothing happened. Or you could control the wind to be so bad your enemies would be blown away."

Logan looked at her with such a frightened gaze that she was afraid to continue. "I'll work with whoever gramps thinks I need to learn from. But why me?"

Morgan hated not being able to answer her son's questions. She couldn't even answer her own. "The grimoire stated that this is passed on to the first-born son of every other generation. We'll learn together. My parents haven't done me any favors by keeping me in the dark about this. I'm sorry. We'll both learn together, but they seem to think this is some special position for you and it's pretty important. I'm curious who this Jadis person is. She's a woman so that makes me even more curious."

"Me, too. I promise to be open to whatever comes of this. I think we need to read all we can before she gets here." Logan stood up when another customer came in. "Thanks, mom." He kissed the top of her head and strode behind the counter.

At the same time, a truck screeched to a halt in front of the store, and she stood to see what happened. Before she got far, her ex-husband came crashing through the door, his hands fisted, and his brows knitted into a scowl. He looked directly at Logan first, then met Morgan's gaze.

"What do you want?"

"First, I'm surprised how quickly your glass door and shelves got repaired. Nice work."

"I know people. How would you know anything about that anyway?" She stared at him, realizing he knew more than he wanted to say. "Were *you* the one who busted everything up? And for what reason?"

"You just need to close this place and come back home where you belong. You've been on your own long enough to know that you can't make it. Go pack your bags and bring them down here. The truck is just outside. You're coming home!"

Chapter 20

"You no longer have any control over me! Get out of my store *now* before I call the cops!" As Morgan stood her ground, her ex-husband suddenly gasped for air as he reached for his throat with both of his hands. He couldn't breathe and was turning red. When his face turned dark red from lack of air, she turned to look at Logan for help.

Instead, what she saw shocked her. Logan was glaring at his father with an angry curl to his lip, his hands fisted, and then his head nodded sideways. At the same time, his father was thrown against the wall and landed on the floor still coughing.

Morgan yelled at her son. "Logan!"

He unfisted his hands and cracked his neck. "He'll be fine, mom." Logan's blue eyes crackled with electricity as he walked over to stare down at his father. "I think you need to leave, now. Mom is *not* going anywhere with you. It's time you started a new life, and it won't be anywhere near her...or me, for that matter. If I see you harassing her again, I'll do more than choke your ass."

His father stood up and glared at Logan, then at Morgan, and back to Logan. His fingers still touched his throat. "What is she? A witch? You saw what she tried to do to me!"

"Get out, dad, before they lock you up for sounding like a lunatic." His father took a step toward Morgan and Logan stepped in front of him. "The door is the other way. Hopefully your truck gets you back home *safely*."

"What's that supposed to mean?"

"Accidents happen. Be careful, *dad!*" Logan walked away. His customers at the counter had just stared at what they saw and shook their heads at his father as Logan made his way back behind the counter.

Morgan wasn't even sure of what *she* had seen. Her ex nearly broke the glass in the door again as he left. When he got into his truck, the stare he sent her way could have killed her. She shook her head as he drove away and turned to watch Logan, shocked that he could have done something like that to his father. The grimoire said his anger could make anything possible. They needed to read the book together and soon.

Nate walked through the back door, and Morgan glanced at her watch. The time was well after five, and Logan had started the clean-up of the coffee machines while the customers slowly made their way out of the store for the day.

"You're white as a sheet, hon. What just happened?"

She waited until the last person had left, then she locked the door and turned the open sign around to read 'closed'.

Nate had turned to Logan while she locked the door. Logan finished the last of the clean-up and wiped his hands. "My asshole father just paid us a visit, and I nearly killed him. He had the audacity to order Mom to pack her bags, that she was leaving with him. I just put him in his place and told him to get out." Logan shrugged his shoulder like it was an everyday occurrence.

"He choked his father with just a look!" Morgan still couldn't believe that her son had that kind of power already.

"Mom, I had no idea I could even do that! All I did was *think* about it and he grabbed his throat. And when I tipped my head, he slammed against the wall and sank to the floor."

"Holy shit, man. Remind me not to make you angry." Nate's eyes were round when he looked back to Morgan. "I think we all might need a drink. I'll drive us to Krazy Locals."

Logan looked at Morgan. "I'm ready. I'll ride along."

"Let me grab my purse. I'll be right down. Want to call Rafe and Kinsley?"

Nate nodded. "I'm on it."

At Krazy Locals, Morgan led the way to the bar inside of the restaurant behind the cafe and took a large table in the corner. The three of them sat down, and Mandy quickly came over to say hi to Logan. Morgan liked her and was glad Logan had someone nice to date for now. If it lasted, she would be happy about that, too.

Mandy smiled, her blue eyes twinkling at Logan. Her blonde hair was up in a messy bun today, like the way many of the younger people wore their hair. She sat down with them. "Lindsey will be your waitress. I'm not old enough yet. Oregon frowns on those of us who aren't twenty-one, but I can take your orders."

"Beer for me, make it two!" Logan reached for her hand and his eyes took in Mandy's face. It melted Morgan's heart that he might be that happy. Since her own heart had found its mate, she only wanted the same for her son. Time would tell.

Mandy took their order and rushed it over to Lindsey.

Morgan looked up to see Rafe following Kinsley toward their table. "Hi, guys! Good to see you. I'm glad you could join us."

Kinsley got comfortable and hung her purse on the hook under the table. "I'm glad you guys called us. I felt something in the atmosphere earlier but wasn't sure what it could be, so I'm hoping you can give me some insight."

Logan looked at Morgan and shrugged his shoulder, giving her permission to explain their incident. Once she did, Kinsley nodded. "That all makes so much sense. I've heard of protectors, but I've not dealt with one. I'm glad he's on our side."

"My father is sending an old friend of his to train with Logan. I'm not sure what kind of training this entails, where the training will take place or anything. He said she would be here next week. Her name is Jadis. By old friend, I envision her as not being able to train a twenty-two-year-old. I guess we'll find out."

"I'm sure the gym will let them use a space there if that's something she might need." Nate glanced up as Lindsey brought their drinks and got them passed out. "Here's to Logan's training next week. Maybe he can teach us a few tricks."

Logan laughed with them, but Morgan could see that the incident with his father shook him more than he wanted to show. He'd stood up for her happiness, and it touched her that he would do that. She assumed he was texting with Mandy.

After a few beers, Logan hugged Morgan, got up and pushed in his chair. "Mandy is taking me back to my apartment, mom. I'll pick my truck up tomorrow. She and I have a lot to talk about. See you later. I know you're in good hands." He gave Nate a wink before he left.

"He's a good kid, hon. Sorry your ex is such an ass." Nate gently bumped her shoulder. "But I like Mandy."

"I do, too." All she could think about was their future and the trials they could both face should they stay together.

Mandy's mom, Katie Parker, joined them at their table and sat where Logan had. "The cafe up front is closed but the kitchen is open for bar patrons. Our special this week is the peanut butter bacon burger. It's been pretty popular, but I'm done for the day. The night cook does a wonderful job." Lindsey brought Katie a spicy clam digger and she took a sip to taste, then gave her bartender a thumbs-up.

Mandy looked so much like her mother it was almost eerie, but Morgan would never say that. If her daughter had inherited all of Katie's abilities, she would be a powerful mate for her son. Katie wore a beautiful talisman on a gold chain with two stones. "I love your necklace, hon!"

Instantly, Katie touched it with her long fingers and smiled. "Thank you! They are clear quartz and black obsidian. They protect me.

Mandy wears them, too. Your Tree of Life necklace is pretty."

"From my mother. I love it. It's amethyst."

Kinsley looked at Rafe. "I'm glad she's protected and has a direct line to her mom."

He agreed. "It's nice we all got together. We need to do this more often."

Morgan agreed. She relaxed as she chatted with her friends. Moving to Pebble Cove was the best choice she'd ever made. But something nagged at her with regards to Kinsley and her office building. "Kinsley, I hope if you have issues in the old basement at your office that you call someone to go down there and not go yourself."

Rafe spoke up as he put his arm around Kinsley. "I've already made that point to her. I'm glad someone else agrees. The vibe I get in the basement isn't a good one, and she doesn't need to be down there alone, if at all."

"I have you to do that, babe, I know that." She patted the back of his hand and smiled up at him. "By the way, we plan to help you put up the wards at Nate's place in a few days. We don't want you going there unprotected."

"Thank you for all you've done. A toast to keeping the evil at bay!" She bumped Nate's shoulder, and his eyes sparkled at her as he held up his beer. Morgan wasn't sure but something wasn't right between Kinsley and Rafe. She left it alone and just smiled, hoping their future would be okay.

* * * * *

A few days later, Kinsley tightened the chin strap on her helmet as she sat on her Harley in the driveway. She hadn't been able to ride as often as she wanted, and today seemed like a good day to see if Stephanie was with Diablo at the Dragon's Lair in Hagstone. The ride would only take about twenty-five minutes, and the fresh air would do her good, as well as the change in scenery with the view of the ocean. She needed time to clear her head.

Slipping on her leather gloves, she leaned forward, jumped on the start, and the engine vibrated beneath her. She carefully made her way down her driveway, the iron gates already opened. Once on the road, she opened it up and on down the highway she rode, getting high on the fresh breeze as she passed the wooded areas filled with pine trees. Those were the scents she craved. She and Rafe usually rode for hours, but he was busy at work today and she wanted out. Diablo would keep her company for an hour or so. Hopefully Stephanie will be there, too.

When she arrived at the Dragon's Lair, Kinsley parked and looked around. She removed her helmet and hung it on the handlebars, undid her ponytail, and shook out her hair as she unzipped her leather jacket. *What a wonderful ride!* Pulling open the heavy door to the Dragon's Lair, she had to re-adjust her eyes to the darker interior. Only one couple sat back in the corner, and she headed straight for the end of the bar where she always sat with Rafe.

"Good to see you, Señorita! Are you riding solo today?"

"I am. It's always good to see you, Diablo. How's your woman? Is she around today?" Kinsley tugged off her gloves and placed them on the bar.

Diablo set a double Jack in front of her. "Not sure if Steph will be by or not, darlin'."

Kinsley pulled out her phone to check messages, hit the jukebox app for music, then tapped the news apps for fun. She would enjoy Diablo's company until Steph came in.

Chapter 21

Kai McGarrett pulled his Harley up to what appeared to be a quiet local tavern in this small town. He enjoyed stopping by the pubs to get a feel for the local folks. There were a few other bikes over to the side, likely belonging to those patrons inside. He had ridden around the area to scope things out and figured the occupants must stick close to their homes and with their neighbors. Most seemed to be hanging out in their backyards. Not many people roamed around this late in the afternoon, even though it was late May, so he didn't have to worry much about having someone come up behind him. He hung his helmet on the handlebars, then removed the key and tucked it in his pocket without immediately getting off the bike.

The homes weren't close together like they were when he lived back east. He liked it out here. Space to relax and not feel closed in. The clouds hid the early moon overhead, lending to the eeriness. His day-long ride along the coast up from California had shown him many small towns spaced out between thickly wooded areas. The road took him near the edge of the cliffs along this region that overlooked the Pacific and the breathtaking views.

Almost too peaceful. Something seemed off. His military training with Special Forces taught him to stay wary, never trust what you see. Being a cougar shifter on top of that always kept his inner feline on high alert.

Through the windows, the dark tavern appeared quiet. Faint music drifted over the parking lot from a jukebox that played Highway to Hell. Just how he liked it. Kicking down the stand, he swung his leg over and off the bike as he took another look around. A small downtown area lay a few blocks up the street. He checked his senses with his surroundings, then slowly made his way to the door.

A shrill squeak sounded as he pulled the door open, and his boot heels sounded on the wooden floor. His skin prickled with an unseen danger as he stepped inside, so he knew he was in the right place. Other shifters hung out here, too. Kai scanned the patrons now that his eyes had adjusted to the dark bar. Three men looked his way for a quick notice and went back to their drinks. A single female at the bar didn't bother to turn around as he walked toward a bar stool.

He made eye contact with the muscled, bear-like bartender, a toothpick in the corner of his mouth, whose eyes motioned for him to sit at the opposite end of the bar from the woman. He glanced to his left at the lone female, then sat where he was directed, first making a mental note that no one sat at the tables in the dark corner behind him.

The bartender, who he'd already sensed was a shifter, stepped over to take his order. Shifters immediately sensed other shifters. "We don't get many strangers in these parts, let alone those coming in by themselves. We run a friendly bar here."

"Sorry to disappoint you. I go most places alone. Double Jack on the rocks, please. Hey, nice notification with the squeaky door." The bartender raised an eyebrow but made no comment. The drink and coaster arrived in front of him, and the bartender stepped over to wash a few glasses. The poor lighting in the place didn't award Kai a good view of the woman who chose to sit alone with what he assumed to be Jack on the rocks.

Good choice.

He took in her appearance over the rim of his glass and wondered why such a beautiful specimen would be alone...and drinking Jack on the rocks. *Guy trouble?* The bartender refilled her glass. She didn't look up and her long dark hair draped over her face, hiding the rest of her appearance. Her head bobbed slightly to the new beat of *George Thorogood's* *"I Drink Alone"* which could have been her theme song. Her slender form fit perfectly into the leather jacket and black jeans she wore beneath her leathers and knee-high boots. Kai knew where else she'd probably fit as his groin tightened. Something that hadn't happened in a while with the life he'd led lately.

Being an investigator kept him busy. Mostly murders where the authorities had trouble nailing down evidence to catch the perp. Being single allowed him to come and go on any job he wanted to accept, and his wild inner cougar wasn't ready to settle down any time soon. A lonely life, at times, but it worked. He hadn't found his mate yet, so he didn't understand the pull toward the woman at the other end of the bar when he had no idea who she was.

As if she'd read his thoughts, the woman's head came up, then sniffed the air in his direction. Her head slowly turned toward him, her long nails brushing back the length of hair, and she met his gaze.

Air rushed into his lungs.

He hadn't seen those glowing green eyes in twenty-five years, and her gaze instantly narrowed on him.

She sniffed the air again. Shadows still shrouded her appearance, but her eyes were unmistakable. He remembered her firm jawline and slender neck; he didn't need to see them to remember the feel of her skin against his lips. The memories of their teenage past sparked his entire nervous system and made his skin tingle.

Kai finished his drink and caught the bartender's attention and nodded toward the female.

The bear of a man looked his way, then over at the woman, raised his brow, and met Kai's gaze. "It's gonna take more than two drinks for you, man, but I'd tread lightly." His drink got refilled, and the bartender leaned back against the middle of the bar as if to watch.

She turned her attention back to her drink and picked up her phone. Her hair dropped back into place.

Kai glanced at the bartender. His dark hair was held back by black material with skull and crossbones, and his arms were well tatted. "You her keeper?"

The bartender laughed out loud, but his comment came in a low voice. "That *babe* doesn't *need* a keeper. Just a word of warning to you."

Kai nodded acceptance of the information. She could only be one person. No one else he'd known had ever possessed those eyes. And no one since her could look at him and make him instantly hard. Not in his last twenty-five years of searching. Even in the dark you saw them...like a panther on the prowl. If his memory served him correctly, twenty-five years ago they'd come so close to having a torrid relationship as teenagers, but it never culminated.

They were both young and carefree at the time, too young to be considering something permanent between them. He wasn't sure what happened, but he went on with his life and never saw nor heard from her. No relationship after her had come close to what they'd shared, if one could call it that. *No* other woman he'd met had kissed like his green-eyed woman back when they were just teens.

Thoughts of her had haunted his dreams during his military years. He'd tried hard to forget her by chasing other women. None ever measured up, and he still craved what could have been. *Why hadn't I ever gone back to look her up?*

The restrooms were on her side of the bar. He'd have to walk past her on his way...what would it hurt to touch her? Would she remember him? Perhaps too much time had passed. He rose and walked toward her as she lifted her head and looked into the bar mirror. Their eyes met in the mirror and hers glowed back at him. Her slender neck begged for his touch…and he couldn't resist the memories of their past nor the warmth of her flesh against his own. So, he reached his long fingers out, meaning only to caress her, but what met his fingertips were glowing sparks of fire like he'd never seen before.

She slid from the bar stool so fast it was a blur. Kai jumped back just in time to avoid a kick between his thighs from her boot, and he grabbed her ankle, feeling the sparking energy through the leather, up clear past his shoulder. None of that had ever happened when he had touched her twenty-five years ago! *What the hell?*

Magick?

Now?

Then again, he didn't know he was a shifter back then either.

Her green eyes still glowed at him, but he held tight as she gripped the chairback for balance and slipped her phone into her back pocket. She moved like a sleek black panther, stealthy and guarded. "If you care to keep that right arm, you'll let go of me. Others before you haven't been given a choice!"

He slowly released her boot, and she took a step back from him, her silken tresses cascading behind her. As her gaze gave him the once over, her eyes narrowed, and her upper lip curled at the side. "It *is* you! After twenty-five years, why are you back in my life, and how did you find me clear over here on the west coast?"

Kai looked at the bartender who shrugged his shoulders and put up his hands. "I warned you, man. You don't fuckin' listen. I'm guessing she already knows that!"

Without looking at Diablo, she agreed with him. "We already know he doesn't listen. This isn't the bar, nor the town, for you to quench your thirst in. Keep moving south, *stranger*. As far south as you can get, if you know what's best." She stepped over to the bar and grabbed her gloves, downed her drink, then spun on her heel toward the door.

He would never forget the sound of her boot heels on the floor, nor the hatred in her eyes...nor the sway of her sexy ass in those tight black jeans. *Damn!* The door screeched closed behind her. Then a Harley started outside and took off into the distance.

What did she remember of their past that he didn't? Why so much anger?

Seeing her again after so many years piqued the memories. Sure, he'd made a mistake long ago and let her slip through his fingers. He'd never met another woman yet who tightened more than his insides the way Kinsley had.

Damn!

Kai used the restroom, and as he walked back to his chair, he caught a scent he was hoping not to. His skin crawled, and his nails itched, alerting him to possible danger. A fourth man had joined the three at the table. Taller and broader shoulders, longer hair, and wicked eyes.

Kai took his seat as the bartender stepped over. Liquid gold filled his glass again. "This one's on the house, man. No one around here *ever* touches her except for *Rafe*. He's the Sheriff. So far, you're one lucky bastard. I've seen her incinerate a man to ashes. She's not someone *I'd* mess with. Just sayin'...I'm Diablo. Welcome to Hagstone Cove."

A chuckle rumbled in Kai's chest, and he leaned toward Diablo. "A witch community?"

"No comment. Safer that way, but depends on who or what you're looking for?" Diablo popped the lids on a few beers and delivered them to the four men sitting closer to the door.

Diablo returned to the bar, relaxed back against the counter and studied him. "Looking for anyone in particular?"

"Sheriff Conley. I'm guessing he's the *Rafe* you spoke of." Kai took a breath in. "Suppose to meet him here this afternoon."

"Then the man will be here. He's always on time."

As he'd ridden through many of the small towns and dark, wooded areas on his way up the coast, this town didn't feel any different from the last two, Ravensville, then Pebble Cove and Hagstone Cove. Each had weird names and a sense of eeriness about them, including the drive through the wooded areas. His cat-like senses had been on high alert while he drove, same as it was now. At least two of the men at the other table were shifters, who had likely realized Kai was one, too. That's just how it was. They sensed each other.

Kai didn't want trouble. He was ordered to the area on a special mission and cursed those above him who thought he'd be *right* for this job. His time in special forces taught him to take orders and follow through, but he wasn't sure he'd be able to with *this* mission.

His spine stiffened as a scent wafted in from outside. Car doors slammed before the screech of the door sounded and pierced his brain. Three tall men in uniform entered and sat at the other end of the bar.

Shifters. All of them

Kai watched as they ordered up sodas. One looked in his direction and their gazes met and held. Kai wasn't looking for trouble, nor would he back down.

He held his glass up in a toast, hoping to remove any interest on the sheriff's part. "Just passing through, boys."

"Good idea, stranger." The sheriff separated from his friends and made his way toward Kai. This had to be his contact person. His higher ups said the guy was sheriff of the town. "I'm Sheriff Rafe Conley. You must be Kai McGarrett? Their description of *you* was right on, but I need some ID just for formalities."

Rafe.

Only Rafe touches her.

Kai pulled out his wallet and handed over his security ID along with his business card as his mind connected the dots. As he watched the man, he wondered what kind of relationship Rafe had with Kinsley, and he'd keep it to himself that he'd had a run-in with her a few minutes ago. "Nice to meet you, Sheriff. I doubt this is the place to have a conversation."

"Correct. Here's my card. I'll be in touch tomorrow, and we can go over the case files. Shit is far from being solved, nor stopped. I hope you're up to a challenge."

"I look forward to hearing from you, sir." Kai put his ID away, gave Rafe a look over, paid his bill, and went to find a hotel in town. Again, his hackles raised as he passed the table of four men. Kai paused, lifted his chin in their direction, but they just raised a beer to him, wanting no trouble, and he left. Damn, his inner cougar needed a night of running. He'd been restrained too long. It could serve as a good outlet to survey the area under disguise.

* * * * *

Back at the station, Rafe Conley tossed his keys on his desk and read over Kai's security card. The guy appeared tough enough for the job. And a shifter at that. Rafe sensed his power before they'd even entered The Dragon's Lair. Mike would not have sent him if the man wasn't qualified. It could all wait until tomorrow.

Hopefully, tonight will be a quiet one. They already had a missing tourist. He didn't need anymore. Perhaps Kai could sense information that Rafe hadn't.

His main deputy and right-hand pack member, Nate, stuck his head into Rafe's office. "I hope that guy has some answers for us tomorrow. He's got good shifter control. I saw it when he walked past Reaper and his bunch. I'm surprised they didn't shift right there in front of him. Those guys have been wanting to do a takeover. Although none of them could take your place as leader of the pack. You know that, right?"

Rafe laughed. "Yes, I do know that. Thanks. I want to meet in the morning with our new guy. I'll let him know Destiny may be back soon. I'm sure he'll want to talk with her, too. See you then. Have a good night." Nate had been his right-hand man for years. Poor guy had been stricken with one blue eye and one green eye, but Rafe didn't even notice anymore. His dark hair drew away from his eye color.

Pack leaders weren't normally fought over but handed down. Unless a guy seriously thought he could take down a current leader and had good reason. Reaper and his gang had been a headache for the department for a while now, and he wished they could just be run out of the area.

If Kinsley wasn't busy tonight, he could use a few drinks. He dialed her number but had to leave a voice mail. He remembered passing her Harley on his way to the Lair and wondered what she'd been up to. Diablo hadn't said a word about her being in there. Maybe she wasn't home yet. That gave him time to make sure all the necessary files were ready for review tomorrow and he locked them in the filing cabinet, then headed home.

Continued in the next book,

Coastal Midlife Magic

More Information

If you'd like to read more about these magickal characters and their friends, be sure to grab your copy of book two, *Coastal Midlife Magic*, and book three, *Coastal Midlife Potions*, of the Pebble Cove Series. Watch for more books in this series by subscribing to Brandi Wilde's newsletter which you'll find on her website:

https://brandiwildeauthor.com

If you enjoyed this book, please consider leaving a review at your favorite online store, GoodReads.com or go to Brandi's blog on her website where reviews can be left in the comments section for each book. She appreciates all of her readers.

About the Author

Brandi Wilde lives in the Pacific Northwest with her husband, a retired captain of the area fire department and previous law enforcement officer. She plots her upcoming books about witches, shifters, and demons in locations around the area. Brandi also writes under the pen name Deanna Jewel. You can visit her website at DeannaJewelAuthor.com. Deanna writes historical fiction, time travel, contemporary, and paranormal romances.